ZODIAC THRONE

WARRIOR SHIFTER BOOK FOUR

R.C. LUNA

To Manuel.

In all the world, there is no heart for me like yours.

In all the world, there is no love for you like mine.

~Maya Angelou

CONTENTS

CHAPTER 1

The thousands of tiny suns at the very top of the massive Underworld cave dimmed as they faded off into the distance. A Zol orb glowed above me and the misty shape of the UnZol King, Balastar Ramon del Castillo.

Carly continued channeling the power of zodiac magic through the orb in order to bring the ancient UnZol King forth from the Void after the kiss that would forever make us Zol Mates. My hands, which had been shaking the entire climb up the side of the pyramid, stopped shaking the moment I made contact with the essence of my Zol Mate, the UnZol King. And all at once, everything felt right. At the moment that my lips grazed his phantom face, I was overwhelmed by a feeling of trust. Releasing myself to trust anyone was an impossibly hard thing to do; every tough lesson I'd had learned in my young adult life had taught me not to.

In the days leading up to the rite, Carly and I had spent a lot of time together. She told me how she had studied all the old scrolls and books about these ancient ceremonies to make sure her rite was executed with precision. She had spoken with awe when she'd described the time the death god Vucub-Cane had gone over all of it with her, taking the time to check her spells, her form and the timing of her movements.

"It is critical that you enter the rite with a truly open heart," Carly had said when she was preparing me for today. "It doesn't matter how the stars brought you here. What matters is that, when you're standing in front of him and make your first contact under the Zol orb, your heart is pure."

"How can my heart be pure when so much corruption has brought me to this point?" I'd asked. All I could think about before the rite was that everything about our mate bond was tainted and toxic.

To start off, the relics—which were created from the body parts of the UnZol King himself—had brought nothing but death and destruction to the worlds of Zol Stria and Earth. Then I got blamed for the destruction of Zol Stria because of a prophecy, got chased, captured and thrown in the Zodiac prison by the death god Hun-Cane. Then his twin brother and also death god Vucub-Cane kidnapped me and now I found myself in a beautiful black dress mating the Unzol King. These were all a series of unexpected chain of disasterous events that kept getting bigger and more elaborate as the days went on.

But Carly insisted that I could find a reason to actually want to mate the ghost king. In those days before she would say, "You must find a motivator that is true for you. Search your soul and find a genuine, honest reason why being mated to the UnZol King, and helping us bring him out of the Void and into this world, is something you want."

Many nights I considered rejecting him. I visualized myself standing up on that platform and refusing to go through with it all. Maybe I would shift into my jaguar form and make a run for it. Of course, Vucub-Cane would stop me in my tracks with his mind control, just like Hun-Cane did right before he threw me in prison. And this is all besides that fact that if I rejected a Zol Mate, we would both be doomed to an eternity of unhappiness in love. It meant I would never find love again and that any relationships I would have would be ill-fated.

But I didn't care much about that. I wasn't going through with this mating bond to avoid a tragic love life. I had managed to have a tragic love life just fine all on my own. No. I was doing this because I didn't want my unit to be punished anymore. I didn't want anyone else I loved to die. And I was hoping that what I had learned about Balastar being a savior for the oppressed was true. Yet none of those reasons were the true motivator. Just beneath the surface, there was something even stronger than all those reasons, and it was what kept my heart pure at the moment that I swept my lips against his.

It must have been the right reason because after we made contact a charge tingled over my skin. My gossamer skirt swooshed as a cool breeze swept around us. Even with the watching eyes of thousands of spectators below, in that instant we were alone.

His kiss didn't linger. Instead, it was the briefest of kisses, but it was enough to commence the return of the UnZol King. In my head I had gotten used to calling him by his real name, Balastar. For whatever reason, it felt more natural that way.

Lights sparked around him, glimmering, and speckled, and they glowed brilliantly as they lit him up from the inside out like a captive star. My eyes grew wide as I watched magic cover him in a glowing sheen. I took a few steps back and tried to keep my mind from racing as it began to sink in that this was all really happening.

Would he fight for the freedom of all people, or just the Dark Zodiac? Would he help me get what I wanted most of all, which was to be free from the command of the death gods?

I wanted all the nagual to live free, not as slaves subject to the whims of gods. Hope for our freedom was the motivator that had brought me to the top of the obsidian pyramid. I knew it would be complicated, perhaps it would even be an impossible task, but if anyone could help me fight for our freedom, it would be my Zol Mate.

As the UnZol King took a step back and blinked at me, the urge to trust him returned. I decided not to resist the feelings stirring for my mate, curious at the emotions that were starting to rise from within my Zol. I didn't expect to feel this happy that he was coming back. It was like I just couldn't wait to see him in the flesh again. It was like this was the greatest thing that could ever happen. It was like fireworks on New Year's and dancing to your favorite song. This feeling of happiness for someone I didn't even know, was strange in my logical brain but not in my body. For a moment, it felt too good to allow myself to worry about it. I let myself trust that everything would be ok, including this.

The unexpected happiness coursing through me began to mix with another feeling. Loneliness rushed to the surface. That was when I realized I had missed him. Deep in my reincarnated soul, I had missed him. A single tear fell from my eye, and my lips quivered in relief as though I had been waiting an eternity for this to happen. His phantom hand reached up and cradled my jaw, unsuccessfully wiping my tear with a shimmering ghost of a thumb.

"Balastar," I whispered. Zol knows why the combination of syllables that made up his name felt more familiar now than they ever had before.

He was still a mystery, and the more I explored the emotions coursing through me, the more I knew they weren't rational. They came from some place deep inside of me. It was a part of me I didn't yet understand.

He shifted his gaze around the platform, reaching his hands out in front of him and opening and closing them as though he hadn't done that in a long time. Then he shifted his blank, unreadable gaze to the Devil's Eye around my neck.

Carly stepped forward and stood between us. She took the Devil's Eye necklace in one hand and swept her other hand over it as she chanted in the ancient language of the Zol Sen. A stream of golden light shot from the Zol orb and the Eye crumbled to ash. Its ashes rose into a tiny, dark-energy tornado that crackled and hummed with power. She opened her palms and channeled the tornado at him. It headed directly for his eyes and funneled right into them. Soon after he became noticeably more of this world than that of the Void. His eyes revealed more depth than they had before, as though there was a Zol in there, somewhere. I looked down, and where the eye-shaped stone had been, now there was nothing except the silver frame that had held it in place.

Carly repeated the process with each of the relics, and with each one he became more alive and present than before. By the time she finished, there was no Blood Ruby on the ring I wore. When I looked at the table, the Obsidian Heart was also gone, along with the Stone Mind and the Blade Bone. The Snake Tongue's sheath was wide open, but there was nothing inside. Every relic had disappeared.

The few Fae on the platform with us bowed before him, me included. I was overwhelmed with awe and my honor compelled me to acknowledge the wonder before me with the bow. Vucub-Cane was the only one who didn't lower his head at the King. Instead, the death god approached Balastar and met his gaze, eye to eye.

"Welcome back," he said simply, and Balastar nodded.

Vucub-Cane cocked his head, and I wondered what the god was thinking. Was that concern on his face?

"Darkness reborn, serve the Zol as one," Balastar said, his voice breaking as though it was a strain to say the words.

"Ah, yes. There you are." Vucub-Cane patted Balastar on the shoulder.

Carly concentrated on Balastar, chanting spells and casting protection wards on him. She had told me he would be at his most vulnerable upon his return, disoriented and confused. In order to stabilize him, she would work a number of spells, all intertwined, to speed up the acclimation of his Zol skin.

Vucub-Cane turned to the crowd with outstretched arms, and the crowd released cheers and hollers. In a voice as loud as thunder, he said to them, "Zol Stria, your god Vucub-Cane has answered your prayers. Today we bring you the Master Zol Sen with the power of a god, the one who is destined to give you your freedom." The death god motioned his right hand to where Balastar stood; his hooded eyes revealed nothing. The crowd hollered and cheered so loudly the trees in the surrounding black forest shook from the commotion.

"He will no longer linger in the merciless Void. This is the time for all of Zol Stria to unite as one. Humans and Fae will live together. The stars write the path." Vucub-Cane took several steps back, and Balastar moved forward.

Somewhere to my left, Carly muttered under her breath, "He still doesn't know where he is. He's been in the Void for far too long." She bit her lip as she studied him.

The crowd clapped and yelled as the UnZol King stood before them. He scanned the mass of Fae in attendance aimlessly, and finally, his blank look gave way to a pinched brow and slight grimace.

Knights of the UnZol Army stood in three long lines at the very front of the crowd. They were dressed in black battle gear with gray armor over the top and the symbol for the Underworld embossed in red over the right breast. As the crowd cheered behind them, they looked forward with concentrated, earnest expressions. They slowly lowered their swords to the side, dropped into a kneel and bowed upon seeing Balastar. The crowd began to quiet shortly after and, row by row, the attendees kneeled as the silence grew among them.

Their loyalty to him after all this time shocked me. It was true, then, that the chosen ones were never forgotten.

"How much longer do we have to be up here?" I whispered to Carly from the side of my mouth.

Her eyes darted to me, then to the death god. She approached Balastar and linked her arm with his. She turned to Vucub-Cane and said, "Your Grace, I must take him inside now to complete the process."

The death god nodded, and she proceeded to enter the enclosed stairs that led down into the pyramid. The crowd released a series of murmurs as he left the platform. I considered following after them—part of me wanted to be sure he was ok—but something kept my feet planted there on the platform, standing before the masses.

"The stars have written that your king shall have a warrior queen as a Zol Mate." Vucub-Cane gestured toward me and I stepped forward. "Fate brings you Queen Sasha. She has been tested and has passed every trial. Her heart is pure. She wants nothing more than to fight for freedom for you all."

Rumbling reverberated through the crowd. After a few heartbeats the faint sound of clapping could be heard, which I assumed was from my unit. The seconds that passed with only a series of low murmurs had me gritting my teeth as my chest tightened. Then the crowd's chattering evolved into a continuous stream of what sounded like courtesy claps. Carly had explained that much of this new generation had only heard legends of the UnZol King and not much about his queen. This made it hard for them to understand who she was, and for the Fae, respect had to be earned. It was never just given. I realized then that there was much to learn about this new role, but more than that, it seemed my work was cut out for me to win over this crowd.

As the murmurs died down, the death god said, "Now, let's celebrate the return of the UnZol King."

With those words, the crowd's cheers exploded.

I released a ragged breath, glad this part was over. Whatever else was coming would have to wait until I'd had at least a couple shots of tequila.

CHAPTER 2

The sconces burned bright orange and crimson as their flames flickered against the dark stone walls of the extensive staircase that led down to the king's chambers. This pyramid had been erected in his honor over two thousand years ago when he'd won the first of the old wars. Shadows whispered all around, tickling my neck and curling around my arms. Our connection strengthened and my skin thrummed as the dark mist charged against it.

I stopped on the stairs and held my arms out in front of me, studying them and the shadows that surrounded me. This was such an incredible sensation; it was as though the shadows were pushing into me with no will of my own. The feeling of it increased as I resumed my descent down the stairs.

My heels clicked on the stone beneath my feet, and with every slow step, the energy from the chamber below felt more intense.

When I reached the bottom and entered the grand chamber, I sighed with relief to find that no one was there. The tables held lit candles and elaborate vases with bouquets of the black, red and charcoal-colored flowers of the Underworld. The arrangements were gifts from the High Dark Fae lord and generals to welcome the Dark King in his return from the Void.

Although my skin was still prickling from the increasing charge of the shadows coiling around me, I took a moment to center myself. I reached for the bond with my shaman, Damian. It had become a habit over the past few years to feel down the bond, reassuring myself that he was there if I needed him. Most of the time I wouldn't say a word and we wouldn't exchange any messages. All I wanted to do was feel comforted in knowing that Damian was just there, within my reach. But this time, I didn't feel him. It was as though there was a huge boulder in the channel between us and there was nothing I could do to budge it.

I'd been briefed that the shaman bond would be severed after I mated with the UnZol King, but I didn't know it would feel this empty without my connection to Damian. We could no longer communicate through our bond and I could no longer reach out to sense his presence and emotions. We had been through a lot together and, despite our rocky start, I had learned to put our differences behind us. Once I had, he'd actually begun giving me decent advice. He'd saved my life more than once, too. He'd brought me back to the palace after I'd almost died from a fight with the hexim. He could have made the Climb out of Xibalba and just left me there to die, but he hadn't. He'd put his life at risk for me.

I guess I was afraid to lose him now, after everything we had been through, and because of the new bond with my mate. I found some comfort in knowing that, although our magical bond was severed, he was still part of my unit. Damian was still family.

The walls began to thrum, black dust and sand shaking from the clay that held this place together and raining around me. I placed my hand on the wall so I could feel the vibration through my touch and try to understand where it was coming from. There was a rhythm: the music and dancing of thousands of Dark Fae just outside these walls as they celebrated the return of their king. It made my head spin that these Dark Fae weren't the enemy like I'd been taught. Or were they?

I wasn't sure what I was waiting for, but I used the time to center myself.

A few hours later I was called into another room, and when I entered, I saw him. Balastar was in the center of the room with Carly seated in front of him and the Zol Sen that wore dark robes sat at his other side. The sleek black furniture was a stark contrast to the gold-and-cream-tiled floor. Ancient hieroglyphic writing with animals and hybrids lined the walls.

"Your recovery from the Void is remarkable," Carly told the UnZol King.

He gave her a smile that was far too confident for someone who had just returned from the endless death in the torturous realm of the Void. "I've been waiting for this for a very long time." His eyes darted to me. "There's my queen."

My chest squeezed at the attention he gave me and I hated it for that. I took a few slow steps forward, still unsure of what bringing back this Zol from the Void meant.

"Come, sit here." Carly stood up and motioned to the chair next to him.

"I'd rather stand," I said, my face blank and emotionless. I didn't know what was going to happen next and I had to be ready.

"I'll leave you to get reacquainted," Carly said with an encouraging nod. Then she strode toward the back of the room to speak with the Dark Zol Sen about something I couldn't hear.

My eyes shifted from her to him, and I caught his eyes staring directly into mine. His lips were soft as though ready to speak, but it seemed he didn't have words. Balastar's eyes were much less frigid now, but they were still otherworldly in the way the pupils expanded and contracted in a haze of darkness as if they had a mind of their own. I could see an emotion revealed in his dark face, but I still couldn't identify it.

I fought to keep my hands from trembling as I bit my lip. My muscles began to tighten, ready to rush out the door. My jaguar shifted beneath the surface, itching to be released. I wanted to run as fast as I could, for hours and hours, until I couldn't run anymore. Something about him scared the shit out of me. It wasn't even the idea of being mated to him. His very real presence before me meant that my life as I knew it was over; there was nothing I could do about it. I was now his mate.

My chest rose and fell with a quickened breath as I felt this unimaginable pull as he looked at me. But that face... his smooth skin against darkened, hooded eyes. My lips parted to speak but my throat felt dry and parched.

My eyes landed on a hieroglyph of Hunab Ku on the wall behind him. This god was referred to as the source of all things. I approached the hieroglyph to study the swirl in the center, very much aware that as I focused on the symbol I was no longer facing him and he could only see my back. The play on colors reminded me of balance. But where was the balance here, in all of this? Here I was, a sworn protector of the very people I was now going to be fighting against. Just a few weeks ago I thought I had finally found a place for myself. I thought I knew who I was. But now I felt more lost than ever.

I was staring at the drawing on the wall when I felt a hand caress my back. A fierce chill ran down my spine. My throat hitched. I jumped slightly at his touch because I hadn't even heard him walk over to me.

"Are you afraid of me?" he asked, his voice low.

Without turning around, I said to him, "They say you don't have a soul. That your heart is as black as tar and as cold as ice. That you created armies of Zolless beasts that leveled cities and feasted on those who didn't have a chance to escape. That you've killed countless Fae and cast a blanket of darkness over Zol Stria in the old wars.

"They say there has never been anyone like you, to have been granted the power of a death god and the command of demons. The only way to stop you from your brutal reign was to slice you apart and confine you to an eternity of torment in the endless Void. So yes, I think it's fair to say that I am afraid of you," I admitted. I regretted the words as soon as they left my mouth. In Zol Stria, emotions were your biggest weakness.

He didn't try to reassure me. He only swept his knuckles gently between my shoulders and down my back, stimulating a shudder to race down my spine. I knew that the mating bond would draw me to him physically. It would make me desire him. At the touch of his hand, I realized it was already starting to happen.

I tried to stop myself from imagining those hands doing so much more, but it was nearly impossible. I took a step forward, putting some distance between us. I turned to face him.

"So is what everyone says about you true?" I asked.

"They would be saying all these things about you, too, if you weren't so good at hiding in the shadows."

My brows cinched. "Ok. I don't understand at all what you mean by that."

"You don't, do you? Still so lost after all this time." He cocked his head to one side as though this concerned him.

He placed his hands in his suit pockets as if he was a billionaire Wall Street investor and not a recently resurrected king preparing for war on Zol Stria. I shook my head. Apparently there were still things I didn't know. And this was entirely because everyone around here spoke in riddles. I relaxed my shoulders, softened my expression and resisted the urge to challenge him. Too many heartbeats passed, and he didn't elaborate on what he'd just said.

"Yes, Balastar. I am completely lost, once again." There was nothing new about that. I wondered if there would ever be a time when I had more insight about myself than those around me. But he wouldn't get the upper hand. I wouldn't let him flip the story to focus back on me. This was about him.

"Tell me something about you that no one else knows," I said. "Something that will help me understand you just a little better."

He looked to the side as he considered what he would share with me.

"My Fae form is a dragon," he finally admitted. "I was the largest dragon to have existed, and I breathed fire. But I'm not sure that's what I am anymore. I can't feel the dragon within me. I feel something else entirely and I'm not sure what it is. I think that's why my eyes are swirling or whatever it is they're doing. The new Fae form is still taking shape within me, and it's very unsettling to not know what I am." He was being sincere.

"I get it. In the years before I came to Zol Stria, I had no idea what I was and it rocked me to the core." Maybe I was starting to understand him a little better. "I don't think I can help you figure out what you are now, but maybe you can help me. Why don't you tell me what you know about me? What did you mean when you said that people would be saying all those ominous things about me?"

"Yes, I promise to tell you everything you want to know." He brought his hand to his heart in earnest and suddenly he didn't seem so scary anymore. "But the story is long and the celebrations have just begun." He held out his hand, reaching for me. "Let's celebrate this very special occasion and enjoy the first night of my return."

I hesitated before placing my hand in his, annoyed he wasn't telling me what I wanted to know.

"Fine. But we will continue this later," I insisted.

"Sí. Of course, we will."

CHAPTER 3

The sounds and movement of thousands of Fae was overwhelming when I stepped outside of the pyramid with Balastar at my side. The adoration from his people was undeniable. His Dark Fae knights were lined up, allowing us a clear passage to the reception through the crowd. The moment the people saw him, they bowed deeply. He reached for their hands, encouraging them to rise and patting their shoulders. Hope was alive in the eyes of his followers.

I spotted my unit in a sectioned-off, tented area where there were lounge chairs and a bar. I immediately quickened my pace to meet them when an Arcana Angel stepped in my path. His mass took up the entire walkway in front of me, and his black, metal armor reflected the light that fell around us. "We will escort you, Your Grace."

To his right was another Arcana Angel, one I recognized as the guard from the prison I'd called Bat Eyes because of his small, shifty black eyes. He bowed his head at me respectfully and I restrained myself from instinctively baring my teeth at him. I lifted my chin and glared at him without blinking. I almost missed the slight tremble of his upper lip, the light sheen of sweat just barely building on his brow.

"You will bend a knee to me," I commanded without thinking twice about it. I wanted him to kneel to the woman he'd kept captive in Xibalba. To kneel and know I was his queen. To show me respect. To know he could not lay a hand on me ever again. And that if he was to serve me, he would need to grovel for my forgiveness.

He blinked twice and glanced around him. It was not lost on me that the crowd had only bowed to Balastar, not to me. I knew that respect for me would need to be earned one person at a time, and right now, I was starting with Bat Eyes.

I parted my lips ever so slightly and released a breath as he lowered his right leg to the ground. His eyes also fell, and he rested his hands on his knee.

"Fine, ok. Get up. Escort me, then," I mumbled out. Despite my asking for exactly this, it was the ceremony of it all that I wasn't used to. So drastic was my shift in status from prisoner to royalty. My eyes darted to my unit as though searching for an escape. I forgot all about how awkward this felt the moment I met Jenna's eyes. She bounced out of her chair at the sight of me and closed the distance between us in six fluttering strides.

"Your Majesty," she said in mock haughtiness. I gave her my most adoring smile and ignored the guard completely as he remained there bowing.

He stiffly lifted from the ground and the two Arcana Angels moved into place in front of me, shifting their gaze through the crowd protectively as Jenna remained at my side.

"There you are. Where's everyone else?" I asked Jenna. She motioned to the tent a few feet away.

"I bet you're glad that's over," she said.

"So glad," I said.

A high general of the Dark Zodiac approached Balastar and they fell into step behind me.

As Jenna and I approached the royal reception area, I found the rest of the unit there. Lex, Andres, Axel, Eliana, Bjorn and Damian were chatting, raising their glasses and joking. I couldn't help but sweep my eyes across the space in search for Zayne. Some part of me still refused to believe that my mentor and trainer, and the oldest nagual of our unit, wasn't with us anymore. I swallowed down the emptiness I felt at the thought of him and found reason to smile in seeing the others enjoying themselves. The handsome king that accompanied me here occupied himself at the other side of the room while I reconnected with my unit.

"Ok, so he's hot," Jenna blurted out as we approached the bar for a drink.

"Mm-hmmm." I pursed my lips as I looked over at him before shifting my gaze back to Jenna. The bartender set down two Narcissus martinis and a bourbon for Lex, who stood on the other side of Jenna. I stared at my martini for a few heartbeats, my mind drifting back to the doubt and confusion I felt about having to mate with the UnZol King.

"Hey, I know that look. Listen, you did the right thing. Ok? If you didn't run into the forest after Trent told you about him and Solana, you may have never been placed in Xibalba by Hun-Cane. And that would have made it much harder for Vucub-Cane to have saved you from an almost certain death dealt to you by the Zol Council, and by association, they wouldn't have let us go either. We all feel the same." Jenna gestured to the rest of my unit. The others nodded in acknowledgment and Bjorn raised his glass.

"Plus, now I have serious doubts about Zol Stria," Bjorn added, shaking his head somberly. "You know, maybe the Dark Zodiac is right. Maybe they do need to be challenged. There's a whole other side to that society that we didn't even know about."

I nodded in silent agreement.

Eliana's eyes fell on mine. "The Zol Council is the real danger. The more I learn about what the UnZol Army stands for, the more I support their cause. Zol Stria is not at all what we were raised to believe it was. The things they do—like taking firstborns into slavery, making outcasts of half-human Fae and taking whatever they want from us—it's an abuse of power. The twelve Houses decided they would rule unchecked and it's time we changed that."

Jenna placed her hand on my shoulder and peered into my eyes. "So don't think about it anymore. It's done and we are going to figure this all out together. Like a family."

The corners of my lips curled upward and I wrapped my arm around her. That was exactly what I needed to hear.

Later that night, the eight of us sat at the top of the pyramid, relaxed and relieved to be alone together. A cloudy mist had formed above us, surely from all the heat coming from the bodies that danced into the night. I leaned my head back against the dark clay podium and gazed up at the tiny suns. At night, they looked like stars in the sky.

"Guys," I asked no one in particular, "how do those tiny suns work?" I pointed to the glowing lights high up in the cave. "They get bright during the day, making it look like sunlight, and they dim at night so that they look like stars. Are they actually suns? How did they get down here?"

Bjorn looked over at me from the wooden table where he was sitting and set down his ale. "You know, I wondered the same thing. One of the females I met at a bar back home had the same suns tattooed up her arm and down her back. I asked what they were and she told me they were just a myth. That the death gods had collected the tiniest suns that had formed at the creation of the universe and placed them in the Underworld to make these impossibly large caves more agreeable to their guests." His voice trailed off as he smiled to himself and took another sip of his ale. "Of course, you have to be brought here by the death gods to actually see that they're real. I always thought they were just a myth."

"So why did she get them tattooed on her?" I asked.

Bjorn chuckled. "If she told me I can't remember. All I remember is what we did next."

Axel, who was sitting next to him, chuckled too. "I remember what she said," he chimed in.

"She said that if the death gods hadn't taken those suns, they would've been absorbed by a larger sun. She got the tattoo to remind her that everything has a purpose, you just have to find it."

"I'm impressed you remembered that," Bjorn said.

Axel nodded, his gaze distant.

"Wait. Were you into her?" Bjorn asked, somewhat surprised.

"Maybe. But she was into you." Axel shrugged.

"I still have her number. I think her name was Rae. Anyway, when this is all over, give her a call. Who knows?"

Axel nodded, considering.

"So how do they get dimmer at night?" I tilted my head and stared at them in wonder.

"Maybe they get even smaller," Jenna said, squinting.

"Maybe they go even higher?" I waved my hand toward the sky.

My head was buzzing from having one drink too many and my mood was lighter than it had been in a while. I turned to face Jenna and pressed my lips together. As much as Jenna told me not to worry about our fate, I couldn't help but think about it.

"Aren't you all sick of doing the bidding of the gods? We aren't tiny suns to be placed up around their backyard like patio lights. We are Fae, just like any other Fae of Zol Stria. Only everyone else has the freedom to choose how they serve the gods but us. Instead, we're forced to do whatever they say and be wherever they want us to be. We can't run away, we can't just decide to not be the Shadow Weavers of the death gods. If we dissent, if we try to run, they will always find us. I hate it." My jaw clenched at the injustice of it all.

"When I learned what I was, I thought it was all pretty cool, until I realized how little control I had over my own life," Andres said, shaking his head.

"My problem is that they drag us into their conflicts. Whether or not we agree with the cause we're fighting for, we have to defend it," Axel said, his voice low. The festivities around the pyramid were dying down. Only soft music could be heard as the stragglers fumbled their way to the sleeping tents that lined the perimeter. "And what's going to happen to us now that the two death gods are divided? Hun-Cane is Team Zol Stria, and we're over here with Vucub-Cane in Team UnZol King."

I lifted my head and shrugged. "Then we need to change it. Nothing is going to change unless we do something about it." As buzzed as I was, my voice didn't slur.

"And how, Queen Sasha, do you propose we start to change it?" Damian asked.

"I'm their Dark Queen." I swept my arms in front of me a bit wider and more exaggerated than I actually meant to, and I gestured to the Fae wandering around at the foot of the pyramid. "So I'll just have to convince my Dark King. Just like I'd like to convince you to cut your beard. It's gotten way too long."

"Really?" He scratched his jaw and looked uneasy. The truth was Damian could do no wrong. He would be handsome no matter how much facial hair he had, but I still didn't like it. "I just wanted to try something new."

"Go back to the short beard you had before. It suited you," I said in my most regal voice.

Damian laughed. "I suppose your new title will grant you some influence on things." He got up from the other side of the platform and walked over to me. He crouched down to meet me at eye level. "We're going to have to be ready. There are still some things I haven't taught you. Some things about the shadows you still need to learn."

His eyes were intent. "War is coming. Now that the UnZol King has returned, it won't be long before we are called to fight. The armies of Zol Stria have grown since he last ruled. They are masters of military strategy and combat. You'll need to prepare." His eyes scanned the others. "All of you."

Bjorn didn't blink and the others nodded their heads.

"We're ready," Andres said.

"If it's war they want, it's war they're gonna get," Axel said, standing.

"You guys... you don't have to keep fighting for me." My eyes drifted to where I imagined Zayne would be sitting if he were with us. "It's ok if anyone wants out. You don't have to do this." It would break my soul to see any one of them go, but it would be worse if they stayed because they felt they had to.

"We didn't come this far only to stop now. Now we have a nagual queen and a chance at freedom. My life is just too long to live at the whims of gods." Jenna grimaced as though a sour taste had filled her mouth. "We do this together, like we do everything."

I wanted to hug her.

The others nodded, eyes sharp and focused. The unit was in agreement. I squeezed Jenna's hand. "Then let's do this."

I didn't go to Balastar's quarters that night like Carly suggested I should. It was way too soon for me to feel comfortable around him. I would keep my distance, resisting the pull of that underlying connection between us that I still couldn't understand or explain to anyone with words.

"Can I sleep with you tonight?" I asked Jenna. She cut her eyes to Lex. He nodded and I smiled.

That night, I borrowed her T-shirt and sweatpants and curled up with her in bed.

"Jenna," I whispered.

"Yeah," she replied, sleepily.

"I can't stop thinking of Balastar. I'm so fucking attracted to him I want to pull him into a room and throw myself at him. It started the second he came back from the Void and it's only getting worse," I confessed. She propped herself up and looked at me attentively.

"Well, he's your mate now. Maybe that's supposed to happen," she said.

"Maybe. But I don't want to give in to that feeling so fast. Too much has happened..." my voice trailed off, not sure what to say next.

"You're thinking too much. It's got to be the mate bond. Just go with it," she shrugged and laid back down.

"I'm not ready." I shook my head.

"Fine, then keep doing what you feel is right, until you are ready," she said.

With that, I closed my eyes. We slept until the afternoon when the suns were once again bright in the sky.

CHAPTER 4

T
he wind swept my hair as Bjorn and I sparred in the arena. An arrow came whirling toward me and I turned too slowly, the arrow just missing my back. Quickly I knelt to the ground, filling my palms with the thin dark clay below my feet. I flung it at Bjorn, but it didn't work. He blocked his face with his arm and avoided my counterattack as arrows continued to rain down on me from the tower above the training arena. Bending and weaving through the shadows, I dodged one, then another, and before I realized it, my skin was cut by the feather of an arrow that barely missed going straight into my neck. *That was too close.*

"Now, Sasha. Throw it up now!" Damian demanded from the side of the arena, his voice sounding more than a little annoyed.

He had taught me a new technique that I was struggling to master. But the arrows continued falling from above and Bjorn was inching closer. He was unrelenting and unyielding and about to grab me in a choke hold which I had no way of escaping from. I had to do something because I sure as shit didn't want to lose this exercise to that massive mountain of a man.

"*Ixil ha,*" I called out as I swept my hands, commanding the shadows to do my bidding. A shield of shadows formed within my palm, crystallizing into a simple obsidian shield to protect me from the onslaught of arrows. Damian had taught me to make the shadows malleable by using enchantments to transform them into physical matter. A single arrow landed in the dead center, cracking the shield like glass and shattering it into a thousand tiny pieces.

"Aargh," I hissed in frustration, but the arrows didn't stop coming and neither did Bjorn.

They wouldn't stop until I was either trapped in his hold or wounded by an arrow. My only reassurance during these drills was that the Zol medics were nearby to heal me before I bled to death. I spun and flipped out of the way as fast as I could so the archers couldn't take aim. It also made it harder for Bjorn to grab me, but after the sixth flip, I was too dizzy to keep going.

I was far enough away now to try conjuring a shield once more. *Focus, Sasha.* Loose strands of hair had escaped my tight braids and clung to the sides of my damp face. Bjorn was only twenty feet away and closing in on me. The sand formed rocks, then boulders that rolled in toward me. He was using his earth elemental power to close me in so I couldn't run or flip anymore. I'd be trapped and the arrows would land on their target. *I have to stop him.*

"*Ixil ha,*" I repeated. This time I formed a spear of dark mist, flinging at him the moment it solidified. He was caught off guard and it pierced his shoulder a moment before he could dart out of the way. I rushed over the rocks that hadn't yet closed me in and ran toward him. He brutally yanked the spear from his shoulder and held back a grunt behind pressed lips. His hands were still holding the spear when I reached the top of the mound. I leaped down and heaved a side kick into his chest. It pushed him backward a few steps but he grabbed my leg as he fell, pulling me to the ground with him. Too quickly for me to react, he wrapped his unscathed arm tightly around my neck and squeezed until my face turned purple. I patted the ground next to me to tap out. He won, again.

I coughed and choked on my breath the moment he released me.

"You're getting better," he said. "This time you drew blood."

A Zol medic approached him and kneeled to the ground by his wound.

"I'm fine," he groaned and stood up. "Let's do this over there." The medic kept his face expressionless as he followed behind Bjorn to the tables at the outside of our training arena. I reached my hand up to my neck. The thick, warm blood that had soaked the collar of my black-and-gray battle gear felt sticky between my fingers.

"You better get that looked at," Damian said as I approached him.

The training arena was inside another one of Vucub-Cane's heavily warded pyramids. The UnZol King's ceremony had been held at a different pyramid made of stone and clay and adorned with ancient hieroglyphics. This one was the complete opposite. It was high-tech and concrete. This was the Deadly Arts Training Pyramid. Above the ground, it was ten floors high and held several more levels underneath. Almost-invisible, frameless glass separated the various training rooms, each occupied by members of my nagual unit. They were being trained by older, more skilled nagual who had left their posts to join the cause of the UnZol King.

"What have you heard about Zol Stria?" I asked Damian after I sat down on a bench. Nearby, the healer was tending to Bjorn's arm with Zol magic. It was healing quickly and didn't look like it would leave a scar. The medic finished and came over to me. I cocked my head to the side so he could tend to it.

"I know that they're preparing for war, just like we are." His voice was grim.

A few weeks had passed since I was mated to the UnZol King and word had spread quickly about his return. Vucub-Cane had been prepared for it, and through an ancient magical ward known only to the gods, he was able to keep his brother out of the Under-world. But we wondered how long those wards would hold and if Hun-Cane had ancient magic of his own that he would soon unleash.

"Hun-Cane keeps challenging Vucub-Cane's wards on Xibalba, and there were a few shadow wraiths that went undetected all the way past the Gray Lands. The Arcana Angel you call Bat Eyes discovered them and took them out," Damian explained. I scoffed and caught his icy glare. He thought I should be over Bat Eyes's treatment of me by now. Damian had said the guy was just doing his job and that I should cut him a break.

"I guess he's good for something, then." My lips curled slightly into a smirk. My thoughts returned to the oncoming war and I got serious again. "Zol Stria seems to be getting anxious. They're gaining ground very quickly."

"And you will be ready," Damian said without blinking.

"I hope so." My eyes turned downward as I remembered what had happened to Zayne.

"More lives could be lost, Sasha. I can't guarantee we will all be here when this is over. The Zol Council doesn't want to hear the truth of it and have refused all our negotiations. The pompous kings and Vicars of Zol Stria are calling this an uprising and rebellion. Their armies are fierce. They have lots of advantages, especially being that they are able to strategize and plan above ground." Damian curled a dark shadow around his fingers. "But we have the shadows."

"Ok, so you just said 'we.' Does that mean you'll join us?" I intentionally kept my voice light, but I was really hoping he would decide to stay on and help us fight. He had a habit of disappearing as soon as his job was done.

"You know why I'm here." Damian pinned me with his eyes.

"Oh yes, I do." He was still after Ixia, and this war promised some hope of him finally taking his revenge.

"And I'll be here until that business is finished." His eyes darkened.

I also wanted him to finish that business with Ixia. She was a narcissist that was only out for herself, and we had gone to great lengths to try and take her down, but she had managed to escape. By some masterful scheming, she'd redeemed herself to the Zol Council.

"Well, I'm glad you're staying," I told him.

Later that evening, I sought solace in the Midnight Gardens around the pyramid. The sky's light dimmed and the tiny suns of the Underworld cast shades of orange and yellow across the high surface of the dark rock. The sight was breathtaking.

Tonight I would be dining with the UnZol King. It would be the first time I'd seen him since the mating ritual. He'd kept his distance. I'd learned from the staff that he spent his days in the war room, preparing for the battles to come. He never came looking for me, leaving me to my training, and I was glad for it. This whole thing was awkward, and by focusing on my training and being around my nagual unit, I could almost pretend we weren't mated.

Except I knew we were mated and there was a whole new set of feelings that arose in me. As much as I didn't want to admit it, I had an urge to see him. As the days had passed after the ritual, my curiosity had grown and I wanted to begin to get to know this man. To learn more about the version of me he'd fallen in love with all those years ago. But I kept these motivations to myself, and whenever Jenna asked me about it, I pretended not to care. The truth was I just wasn't ready to face it.

Carly insisted that we meet for all kinds of celestial reasons that she tried to explain to me, but I was too nervous to understand. She rattled off arguments, like the need for our mating bond to take hold before the next new moon so the very fabric of his existence in this realm could be secure and blah, blah, blah. She also said something about how our bond would finally allow me to tap into the wisdom of my ancestor. I could achieve even higher levels of powers, abilities and skills and hold the memories and experiences of my ancestor in my mind as my very own. That part made my ears perk up just a little bit more.

As she would buzz around me explaining all of this, I would busy myself polishing the blades I kept in my belt or throwing daggers at targets over sixty feet away. At one point when she began to annoy me I shifted while she was in mid-sentence, snarled at her and ran off. She didn't bring it up again after that.

But I couldn't put off meeting with him any longer. The thing was, I had to get clear on what it was that I was avoiding. The happiness and aching loneliness I felt when he first returned scared me. It was time to face those emotions head on and besides, I needed to start moving forward on my plan to free the nagual from the grip of the death gods.

Tonight, we would finally come face-to-face alone.

CHAPTER 5

The fabric of my Oscuri-made dress was a vibrant jade. Senai, the Oscuri Elf Master Designer, had created it to remind me of the endless green palms back in Miami. It was the city of eternal sunshine and I missed it terribly now. That life seemed thousands of years away, not just four. So much had happened since then. And yet, so much of that life made much more sense now that I had discovered who I was. A discovery that seemed endlessly evolving.

Back before my transformation into a nagual, there had always been this undercurrent of energy, this knowing of a presence much different than my everyday experience offered that both confused and terrified me. And back then no one, including myself, believed in this kind magic, or that a world like Zol Stria even existed. To us, magic and its creatures were a thing of myth and legend. How very wrong we'd been.

I climbed the long staircase up to the third level of Vucub-Cane's grand palace. Dinner would be held in a balcony overlooking the Midnight Gardens. There was a whole other kitchen on this level where the demon chefs were creating their masterful five-course dining experiences. The palace servants were all the most skilled, loyal demons of the Underworld. And ever since I'd arrived, the chefs' culinary skills had challenged all my gastronomic preconceptions, far surpassing anything I had ever had on the other side of the Gates, and that was saying a lot because the food in Zol Stria was nothing short of divine.

"That smells incredible," I couldn't help but say out loud as I passed the kitchen and entered the large balcony where a table was set for us to dine. The idea of enjoying that amazing food made me almost look forward to sitting across from Balastar.

"It does smell incredible," a male voice said.

I shifted my gaze around the terrace until I saw him emerge from the shadows at the other side of the entryway. I had scanned the area as I always did when I entered a space and hadn't seen him. Could he shadow weave like me? He probably could, considering how powerful everyone said he was. I took in his dark-blue designer jacket and fine, white, button-down shirt. They made him seem more human than monster.

"You know, Vucub-Cane should have just promised me one of his demon chefs for eternity in exchange for completing the mating bond with you. I wouldn't have put up such a fight." As soon as I made the joke, I realized how awkward it sounded. I shuffled my feet. This king of malice and darkness wouldn't get my sense of humor. Was there any sarcasm like mine those many thousands of years ago when we'd been together?

He took a few slow steps in my direction, looked at me as though he was about to say something, then cast his gaze over the balcony and into the dark night. He didn't laugh or respond to my poor attempt at small talk. The bodice of my dress felt too tight all of a sudden, which surprised me because Senai had an otherworldly skill of creating exquisite dresses of extreme comfort.

It must be my nerves. Calm yourself.

I thought the Zol Mate bond would have called to me. I thought it would make me desire him above all other things in my life and consume me, much like the relentless and unexplainable control the Dark Vampire's bite had had over my emotions. But instead, I was only nervous around him. Nervous because I wanted him to want me for reasons I still couldn't understand. But it was the truth. I wanted a certain, unrelenting heat to simmer within him. A heat that only I could satisfy and one that would eventually lead to my influence over him so that I could get exactly what I wanted out of this whole thing. And as I watched him look out on the Midnight Gardens, I stilled myself with a breath because it had dawned on me why I was nervous.

I saw cold power in his eyes.

He was all business. Was he only here as a chore, because Carly made him do it? I moved to stand next to him. He didn't utter another word as we both just stood there looking out at the black-leaved trees and bushes below. I heard rustling behind us and noted our demon waiter had arrived. He was holding a bottle of wine and two glasses.

"Your Grace, this wine is for your first pairing," the waiter said to me. He poured the white wine and set it down on the table in front of me. I swished it around and sniffed, soaking in the flowery aroma. The wine burst to life against my taste buds.

In a moment like this, a Fae male that was interested in me would have looked at me. Would have watched me drink the wine with some level of satisfaction. Some interest in my own pleasure. But Balastar was far away. He was deeply distracted, and I decided to ignore that.

"It's wonderful," I said. "Thank you, Dimitri."

He poured a glass for Balastar and handed it to him, then finished filling my glass. Dimitri left the bottle in a wine bucket next to the table and went to the kitchen.

Balastar turned to me and reached for a lock of my hair. He twirled it gently in his fingers, studying it carefully. His eyes softened as he took me in and he didn't seem so cold anymore.

Just then Dimitri emerged with two small plates.

"This is your first course. Liquid olives," Dimitri said, placing the plates on the table and walking away.

"Shall we?" Balastar swept a hand to the table and pulled out a chair. He stood behind it expectantly.

"Such a gentleman," I breathed. After I sat, he joined me. Again, the bodice felt tight. I lifted my gaze and noticed that his eyes wouldn't land on me for more than a heartbeat. His mind seemed far away.

The light, liquid olive popped deliciously in my mouth, coating my tongue with a tart caress. I lifted the wine glass to my lips and whispered the tiniest of purrs as the wine saturated my tastebuds.

"You really enjoyed that, didn't you." Balastar's voice snapped me back to the dinner table.

I had forgotten myself in the bite and had begun smiling. When I felt his eyes upon me, my lips tightened again.

"Oh, yes, well Chef Amir is my all-time favorite." My face softened once again and I straightened, looking forward to the second course which would be coming out momentarily.

"You always did enjoy food so much," he said casually.

"Will you tell me more about who I was back then?" This had been on my mind for so long. Now that he'd offered up a little piece of information, it seemed as good a time as any to ask.

"I can't tell you your story without telling my own."

I shuddered. The legends of Balastar were written into the fabric of Zol Stria. The fact that my story was such an integral part of our world's history was hard for me to even imagine. I brought my napkin to my lips and our plates were cleared by Dimitri. The second course, red peppers with garlic and oil, appeared in front of us.

"This may come as some shock to you," he continued, "but Vucub-Cane is my father. I am the result of his coupling with a Dark Fae. She died when I was young, and the Master Zol Sen of Vucub-Cane's palace took me in. They don't gossip, they don't judge, and given that I was the son of a god, they thought it best to raise me as one of them. Hun-Cane had always been against that sort of thing. Vucub-Cane knew his brother would have me killed, just as he'd done to my bastard brothers and sisters."

I placed my fork down and focused on him, forcing myself not to look surprised.

"My mother was a Dark Mage who lived for many years in the human world. Over the years, the demon servants and the Zol Sen shared pieces of her story with me. They say that when she was pregnant, she begged Vucub-Cane to save me from the same fate, but he resisted. She swore to him that I was meant for great things. She showed the Master Zol Sen who'd taken me in readings of tea leaves, bones and tarot cards that all proved I would change the world."

He chuckled to himself as though amused by the distant memory of her. "The Zol Sen told me that during my birth she was able to hide me for a little while in the shadows, but then she got very sick and went to Vucub-Cane with one final prayer before her death. That was when Vucub-Cane decided to help her hide me." He lifted his glass to his lips, allowing me enough time to soak in what he was saying.

"Wow, so you're a demigod."

He simply nodded and set his glass down.

"If Vucub-Cane didn't care what happened to his other bastard children, why did he care about you?"

"He didn't at first. But then, when I was a boy, there was an incident at our monastery. It was an accidental experiment that the Zol Sen were doing on those beasts, the cihauti. Just like the one you hunted. I was a very young apprentice when the Zol Sen Masters had removed the fetus of one of the captured creatures to study it. As the living fetus was lying on the table, a Fire Fae female barged in. Her child had been stolen by the cihautl and, in all her rage, she set fire to the infected creature. That was when the first vision from the cihautl was ever seen; it was of me coming to power and leading a rebellion against Zol Stria. The vision was of a rebellion that I would lead in the distant future." He tilted his head as though choosing his next words carefully.

"My father is always trying to outdo his brother. They've always been very competitive and they have some sort of ongoing battle for power or world domination. Vucub-Cane is an ambitious god and I believe he wants for all of the Underworld to worship only him.

Once he heard about the vision of my rule, he knew that through me, my power, and the power of the legions of Dark Zodiac, he could corner his brother into submission. He would only have to wait centuries to do it. Gods are much more patient than the rest of us, you know."

My eyes flared in surprise and I quickly reined in the shocked expression on my face. I took a sip of my wine as I tried to absorb what I was hearing.

"As I grew and my power expanded, Vucub-Cane realized that the deflector spells and obscuring magic wouldn't work to hide my scent from his brother. So, he called in a favor to the moon goddess, Awilix. She was also a god of the Underworld who allied with Vucub-Cane. He granted her lands in the Underworld and domain over certain deaths and sicknesses in exchange for her help."

The third course was now before us: seared scallops in garlic butter garnished with Italian parsley and pancetta. I was momentarily overwhelmed by the smell and appearance of the plate and my taste buds sprang to life with the flavors of the first bite. Balastar seemed to be enjoying the food as well, taking care to place a cut scallop on his fork before bringing it to his mouth.

"So how was it that Awilix could help Vucub-Cane hide you?"

"As the goddess of moonlight, she created the shadows, the deepest shadow of all being the other side of the moon, which she hid from the sun. It was from those shadows, and her command over what can be hidden from the stars, that your kind was created. You were born on the day of the jaguar, of a line of noble warriors that protected the shamans traveling through the Gates of the Zodiac between the human and Fae worlds. Your family was a loyal patron of Vucub-Cane and served him in his palace. Because of your Aries natal chart, they knew you would be strong enough to yield the shadow. And you were. They gave you to their god in offering, and you covered me in shadows for years, protecting me. Even when they severed my limbs and condemned me to the Void, you never gave away my true identity to Hun-Cane. Until this very moment, I'm not sure he even knows that I'm his nephew."

His cold eyes now glimmered with a hint of admiration for me. My eyes grew wide and I stifled an all-out laugh. All that came out was a low chuckle. It amazed me to even consider that I, with all my flaws and insecurities, had protected the most powerful Fae to have ever lived all those many years ago.

"You find this funny?" He sounded just the slightest bit hurt.

"I find this outrageous." It was a nervous laugh, actually. I dabbed the napkin against my lips and reached for the wine bottle to pour myself another glass. Before my fingers could grip the neck of the bottle, Dimitri appeared out of nowhere and poured wine for the both of us.

Dimitri shot me a comforting glance that set me at ease. My brows cinched in confusion and he nodded softly, as though reassuring me that Balastar could be trusted. Then Dimitri tucked his chin and whirled away as quickly as he'd come. The house staff was loyal only to the god Vucub-Cane, and all the secrets they learned in these walls were preserved by them. Their trust was never questioned, not in their centuries of service to their death god. I wondered then if Dimitri knew this story, too.

"Who knows this story?" I said, tracking Dimitri as he left the terrace.

"Only Vucub-Cane and his closest confidants. I expect Chef Amir, Dimitri and the other demons of the palace would know much of this story, although I've never asked them directly. But they have all been here since the beginning. I expect they know everything I've told you plus everything that has happened since I was in the Void."

It amazed me the layers of secrets at play. I had already resigned myself to never being able to fully understand the complexity of this world of spirit and power, light and dark, stars and fate.

And yet now another secret had been revealed.

One more truth had been spoken, and with it I found one more unraveled thread of my life lying before me.

CHAPTER 6

"Let me get this right. The death god Hun-Cane is your uncle, you're the son of his brother Vucub-Cane, and a Dark Mage is your mother. Your father worked with another goddess to create me—a goddess who commands darkness and shadows—to protect you and hide you from Hun-Cane."

He nodded—a bit too casually, in my opinion. I smirked, amused with the wild direction this was all going.

"So tell me, great UnZol King, when will we get to the part where I became your queen? Was it love at first sight or did you pine over me until finally making a move?"

A small grin formed on his lips. I couldn't believe it. The great UnZol King could smile.

Another course appeared before us: lamb chops soaked in rosemary and thyme, served with a truffle risotto. Chef Amir masterfully paired this course with a full-bodied Tempranillo. My senses came to life with each plate, and my energy remained light and positive. I was comfortable in my dress and felt myself letting my guard down with Balastar as our dinner progressed.

There are all sorts of myths about why you can't eat food in hell. When Persephone was brought to the Underworld by Hades, Zeus had told her not to eat anything as the food would bind her to the Underworld forever. I had been in the Underworld for weeks now, and I wouldn't be surprised if Carly had put something in this food to make me open up to Balastar and help with the binding magic she kept nagging me about. I considered this as I filled another fork with tasty morsels and wished I'd have thought about it earlier.

Oh well, it's too late now.

I took another bite and closed my eyes in delight as the savory texture coated my tongue.

"My Queen, legend has it that you pined over me. For quite some time, actually. You pined when you floated over me in the rafters. You pined while you cloaked my true identity in the old wars. And you pined over me while I slumbered and Nightwalker Assassins came for me. You, Dark Queen, were the one who pined."

I fought the blush that wanted to warm my cheeks. I didn't even know why I was blushing, because that'd been another me. That wasn't at all the woman I was today. Although, I couldn't blame ancient-me for pining. This man was exactly the kind of man any woman would pine over.

"Sorry to say, but I don't trust whatever it is you're telling me about how our relationship went down. Because you're making it seem like this was entirely one-sided and I just don't see myself doing that." I raised an eyebrow, bringing the wine glass to my lips for a sip.

"All those years ago, I thought you were the most beautiful, elegant creature to have ever lived. Now, even after all those centuries apart, I feel exactly the same."

I choked on my wine, nearly spitting it out all over my food.

"Well... I... didn't expect that," I managed to mutter after I composed myself. He had ignored me for the past two weeks, and anytime I may have come across him in passing, he'd barely look in my direction. His indifference to me had convinced me I was the last thing he was interested in.

A breeze shuffled the leaves of the trees just outside the terrace, bringing the fresh scent of rain on rocks with it. At the death gods' command, magical vacuums kept the air flowing in this massive underground cave system at all times.

"Is it because I'm your Zol Mate? Is it the stars that make us want each other and feel that way?" He didn't have to truly love me if we were Zol Mates. The way I saw it, that was just the celestial planets forcing him to have these strong, compelling feelings for me. Not because he genuinely had them. It was the same for me. It was the stars that made me think of him all the time. After I lay in bed, it was the stars that had me imagining his hands caressing my bare thighs under the sheets. That wicked Zol Mate curse was the reason I couldn't think about anything else but him.

"So you do want me." His lips curled.

"Was that all you heard me say?" I sighed.

"No. I don't know so much about Zol Mates. I know they say that's what we are and that there's so few of us it really hasn't been studied. All I know is I'm very happy with the way our mating worked out. I mean, you could have been a hexim or a Zolari Troll, after all. Lucky for me my Zol Mate is a sexy nagual." He chuckled, and I laughed with him.

"I guess you're right. Thank Zol you're not a minotaur or a siren. That would've complicated things for sure." I was still enjoying the fact that he'd called me sexy. If he found me sexy, then that was my way in to start working on him to free my unit and me from the control of the death gods. Besides the fact that it rose in me the desire I kept trying to push down and hide from him.

Tell me what you're thinking, he said without moving his lips.

"Wait, what? Are you in my head right now?" My eyes widened.

Yes. We can speak to each other through the mate bond. Like you did with Damian.

"Oh right, they told me about that." I set my fork down and the plates were whisked away by Dimitri. He returned a moment later with a lemon tart and fresh silverware. "I still don't feel like I know you well enough to talk through the bond, though."

"We can fix that easily. What else do you want to know?" He cut into the lemon tart and took a bite; his eyes glimmered ever so slightly with pleasure.

"Why haven't you spoken to me for the past two weeks? What's been going on?"

He cut me a sideways glare then returned his attention to the lemon tart, taking another bite before answering. "At first, I was getting acclimated to this body and I wasn't sure how to interact with you or with anyone. I wasn't myself. I also began discussions with the generals on our war efforts and it kept me busy until I was ready enough to set up this dinner."

"Ok. Fair enough." It was all I could manage to say before taking my own bite of the lemon tart. "But if I am your queen, I thought I would be consulted on the war strategy. Especially considering my unit's direct involvement with the retrieval of the relics and otherwise being the catalyst to this whole dynamic." My nostrils flared slightly as my frustration began to raise my fire element.

"Sasha." He placed down his fork and pinned me with his eyes. "I didn't ask you to dinner to upset you. I invited you to thank you. I know that you sacrificed a lot to become my Zol Mate and bring me back from that contemptible Void. Your sacrifice means everything to me and my people. I won't forget what you did for us."

He was being sincere. It unnerved me and my guard slipped a little, fire turning to warmth in my veins.

"You're welcome, but seeing as I didn't have much of a choice, I don't really know if you should be thanking me. They threatened to kill my unit, you know." The heat from my fire element returned, stirring in my chest and singeing my fingers at the thought of what could have happened to them if I hadn't agreed to the rite.

"My father's approach left much to be desired, I agree. Nonetheless, I am in your debt, Sasha. You should know that." Something about his tone, the smoothness of his voice, cooled the growing fire within me.

"That is honorable of you, Balastar." I softened to him. "I will have you know that my nagual unit means absolutely everything to me. I feel exactly the same for them now as I did before you and I were mated. It changes nothing that I'm your mate, or that I'm queen. I am still a part of that unit."

His expression remained unchanged as if that was no concern to him.

"And since you say you are in my debt, then I have one thing to ask of you. One very important thing."

"I didn't expect you to call in my debt so soon." The corner of his mouth lifted in amusement.

"Yes, well, it's important. Me and my unit, and all of the nagual that have ever existed and those yet to come, must be freed. We cannot be bound to the whims of the death gods, to be commanded and taken from our friends, families or any other commitments against our will. I want us to be free to choose who we serve and how we serve them."

His smirk was gone and his lips now formed a straight line. "That's not something I can do. The gods created you. They are the only ones who can change your soul contract."

"Then help me convince the gods to give us our freedom. Surely you have negotiating power. Vucub-Cane wants something from you, doesn't he? He wants more power. He wants to overthrow his brother, at least it seems like he does. And you're the key to giving him what he wants. So, he should give you something in return." I locked eyes with him and leaned forward in my chair. He shifted his stare to the right of me, out over the terrace and into the darkness beyond the palace. The soft sound of a cave-dwelling Zolari Owl broke the silence.

He was silent for far too long, and I needed answers. "Well?"

"I'm thinking about it."

My heart raced. *I didn't get shot down. That wasn't an outright no.*

"Even if I convinced Vucub-Cane to release you, there is still the trouble of Hun-Cane. He will be out for your blood the second you leave the Underworld. After all, the prophecy said you would bring me back and that sent the Zol Council on a hunt for you. He'll pick up your scent when you leave Vucub-Cane's wards. This has been part of our discussions in the war room. Although we could use your help in our defenses, we've decided that you will be safer down here once we begin our attacks."

"That's exactly the reason you should push for our freedom! Because if we are free from the control of the gods, Hun-Cane won't be able to control us. We are the only Fae who can shadow weave and we can use this to ambush the Council." I leaned back in my chair, confident in this obvious solution to his problem. "You'll have the benefit of the superior nagual fighting skill with the element of surprise on your enemy. I think it's a win-win."

He fell silent again, staring at me as if he wanted to believe in me.

"This is a proposal worthy of presenting at the war room. Of course, there is the fact that I'm not sure if Vucub-Cane alone can release you from your bond to the gods."

"Well, then I've got to get to work." I stood from the table abruptly. I had already formed a plan to make this happen and now that he was behind my idea, I was anxious to get started.

"What are you talking about? We haven't had after-dinner drinks yet." Balastar swept his hand toward Dimitri, who was approaching us with two brandy glasses filled with a deep-burgundy liquid.

"I'll take mine to go, thank you very much." I reached for it and winked at Dimitri as I strode away.

"But where are you going?" Balastar sounded surprised.

"I'm off to the library. Did you know that the library here is filled with copies of all the old texts, the forbidden chronicles and every banned book ever written? If the history of the creation of ancient nagual is anywhere, it's here. In the palace library."

I loved visiting the palace library. My hands opened wide in excitement, slightly spilling the drink in the glass I was holding, as I marched toward the terrace exit. *I'm going to find the spells that were used to bind the shadows to me and find the way to unbind us. I'll see if I can get Damian to help me do the research. He would know what to look for.*

I stopped briefly to take a slow slip of the Sambuca, then glanced at him over my shoulder. "You should come help me. It will go a lot faster. How good are you at doing research?"

"Wait." He stood up and closed the gap between us in a few quick strides. He placed his hand on my shoulder; his fingers resting on my collarbone felt warm on my skin. My breath caught.

"I still haven't agreed to this." His tone was low, his words were direct but his eyes were smiling with intrigue. "I make no guarantees."

The part of me that responded to his touch just wanted to melt in his arms and accept any fate he wanted for me. But I pushed past his predatorial charm, because charm was the most corrupt of all magic. I knew that game all too well by now. No one would bend my will again; I wouldn't let them.

I turned to face him, sure that the fire was bright in my eyes.

"I just gave you a golden unicorn." My voice was sultry and calculated. "You and your war generals will see that this is the only way you stand a chance at defeating the great reign of Zol Stria. This is how you'll win the war. If you want victory, if you want to be regaled as the great Fae King who brought freedom to his people, you have to start with your fucking mate. It starts right here and with me. My freedom, and the freedom of your people, it is one and the same."

His chest heaved as he sucked in a deep breath, and I knew my words had taken root.

"Well then, we better get started."

CHAPTER 7

My high heels slowed my pace and so did the exquisite food and drink that was settling in my stomach. I couldn't walk down the three flights of stairs and then down the long corridors to the palace library fast enough, so I set down my glass on a hallway table and shadow wove. I became the dark mist that covered me in darkness, coiling around my arms and legs until we were both one and the same. In the time it took me to fade into this dark element, I wondered if the UnZol King would fade into the mist and weave with me. I wondered if he could.

Instead of propelling myself forward toward the library, I reached for the ceiling and lingered there. I watched Balastar from above. After all, he'd said I'd pined over him as a shadow from the rafters. I might as well see what it felt like to do it now, if only for a few heartbeats before he realized what I was up to. If he even realized it.

From above, I could see his silken hair resting thick on his head. He had gotten a haircut since emerging from the Void, a more modern style where the hair didn't reach his shoulders but was still long enough to look sexy. He stopped in his tracks the moment I faded away, sucking in a breath past his teeth in frustration. He ran his long golden fingers through his hair, darting his eyes to where I'd been standing. Balastar took a step forward, hesitated, and released a low chuckle.

Come out, come out, wherever you are.

The UnZol King looked up, directly at me as though he could see where I was lurking above him.

Get out of my head!

I was trying to concentrate. Balastar had said that back in my previous life with him I had cloaked him in shadows. That was different than normal shadow weaving since I used the technique mostly for getting from place to place. I didn't hold myself still in any one location for long, unless I was eavesdropping or spying whenever I wanted the edge on a mission I was working on. But I didn't know if I could also protect someone in this form like ancient-me had. If I could hide things. This was a new revelation of my powers and I wanted to learn more about it.

I darted toward the end of the hallway, sweeping dark tendrils of myself over Balastar. The charge of our connection was instant. He didn't flinch, but I felt every dematerialized part of me dance excitedly on contact. There was a large blue vase right before the staircase which I hid behind and watched as Balastar approached. A predatory look flashed across his face as though he would catch me at my own game.

I can't believe you remembered our game, he said into my mind as soon as he stood before me.

I slithered up the walls and spread out in front of him, trembling a little because I remembered something, I just didn't know what.

This. You used to hide and I would try and find you.

Is that right? I said playfully, wanting him to think I'd known the whole time.

Yes. Now that I've found you, remember what else you used to do?

When he stiffened his shoulders and pulled them back, some primal instinct drew me to them. I crept toward him, hesitating before folding over myself as I draped my inky darkness across his shoulders. Another memory stirred; I had done this a thousand times before. I swept myself around him, curling around his torso and looping around his arms. This contact with him charged me in a way I hadn't felt before, at least not in this life.

So you do remember.

I guess I do, I realized, surprised.

He began to descend the stairs, me clinging to his body and my dark mist cascading behind him.

Where are you going?

To the library, of course.

Of course.

The sphinxes lifted their eyes to Balastar as he entered the library. I clung to him tighter, thrilled with this new ability and curious if others could see me. From the surprise in their eyes, the wonder at the novelty before them, answered that question. I materialized into my Zol skin, clothing in place, but my hair, which had been previously been combed in place perfectly, was now loosely and falling over my shoulders.

As the keepers of the library, the sphinxes approached to give us a riddle to solve in order to enter. The UnZol King may be Vucub-Cane's son, but the sphinxes didn't care. He had to solve the riddle just like everyone else.

Her voice was low and echoed unnaturally, as though her language was of the mind and the words that came out were only for our sake:

You sweep my heart into the sun and turn back time

I didn't expect you but still you arrive

The dead come alive at your will

Yet you can cover my cheeks with tears

You wind straight through my heart, making secrets and desires reappear

Balastar turned to look at me, his eyes revealing nothing.

"What do you think it is?" I asked him.

"Oh, I absolutely know what it is. When you're as old as I am, you know all the old riddles."

I shifted on my feet. I liked a challenge and didn't want him to just give me the answer. "Every time I come here, these riddles seem like they cut right to the core of what's going on in my life." I twirled a silken lock in my fingers, searching the domed ceiling for my answer and knowing I would never find it there. "In fact, this riddle sounds like you. It reminds me of you."

"As it should." He smirked, not giving anything else away.

"Oh, I thought there was a hint coming my way." I gave a little pout of disappointment.

"Not a chance."

I tilted my head to the side, enjoying this playful side of the UnZol King. Seeing him like this surprised me, even though talking to him this way was somehow a distant, hazy memory.

"That's it... The answer is memory," I said, brightening.

The sphinx's expression remained unchanged, but she turned and flapped her large falcon wings and returned to her work.

"You were always good at riddles," he said.

"Was I?" I resisted nudging him with my shoulder, considering I was beaming.

He lifted his chin, his gaze roaming over the silent shelves of books that circled a spiral staircase, first up toward the brightly lit stained-glass dome then down to a seemingly endless dark depth below. "Where shall we begin?"

"This always begins with you, Balastar. Somehow you were the catalyst for so much change. First we begin searching for any texts where you're mentioned, then we'll have to go to your origins, around the time when you were first born. That will be when Vucub-Cane would have decided to protect you from his brother's sight. We need to know when in time that happened to find any instances of connection between you and the goddess Awilix. We'll need to cross-reference that with any texts written by the Zol Sen on the use of shadow magic and the creation of the nagual. There we may find the exact spell we are looking for. That's how we uncover the truth."

Balastar rubbed the back of his neck, seemingly overwhelmed by the work I had explained.

"What? What's wrong?"

He took a step closer to me. I was hyperaware of my urge to reach for his hand, and I desperately wanted him to drape his arm over my shoulders.

"There's an easier way."

"Ok, and what's that?"

"Follow me."

CHAPTER 8

He led me down three flights of stairs, then down a long hallway with three large, engraved wooden doors.

"These are the Guarded Three. They are rooms that shift. One day you'll open a door and enter a certain room, and the next day you will open the same door, and another one of the three rooms will be behind it. These rooms hold the spells of the gods. They're not accessible to anyone that is not a god, unless you have someone like me with the blood of a god."

"Oh, ok. So you're telling me I was going to come up against a dead end, or a closed door, doing research my way." I pinched my lips but softened to him. I didn't expect him to be helping me so fast.

"Yes. And we have spell trackers that archive spells and their creators. There are Zol Sen who specialize in this kind of research. They categorize each and every spell ever heard of, and they send in special agents that uncover the source to create a historical record of their use and evolution. Spells often build off the foundation of others and we can get to the source code spells in the archives. This palace has a duplicate of their records. The Zol Sen Master Citadel is located in Aquarius Gate, but the gods each receive their own master copy for their respective libraries. So what you seek should be found within these doors." A strand of his dark hair fell forward and covered his eyes. He seemed less intimidating down here and more approachable.

"You know you sound much more like a professor and much less like the infamous UnZol King when you talk like that." I placed a hand on my hip, grateful for the chance to bypass a lot of useless searching. "So how do you know which door to open if they're always changing?"

As if in answer, the door on the left creaked open, revealing a bookshelf lined with thick leather-bound books with golden lettering.

"I just have to think of what I want, and the door that holds the information will open." A satisfied look flashed across his face as he admired the open door.

I gave him an appreciative smile and started forward eagerly. "Will the book simply fly off the shelf at your will also?"

He nodded. "One of the many benefits to being the son of a god. Now hold on, you don't want to just saunter in." He placed a warm hand on my bare shoulder. Every other part of me suddenly felt cold. "Let me go in first. We don't know what's behind those doors and I'm not sure if anything has changed about the wards."

"You know, it's nice that you want to protect me and everything, but I'm pretty good at protecting myself," I huffed.

"I have no doubt," he said, and walked past me inside. The door closed behind him and directly in my face.

I frowned. "What just happened?"

Looks like they still won't let you in if you're not a god. Just wait out there.

I turned around and paced the hallway. There wasn't much to look at except the intricate engraving on the doors.

A book fell off the shelf right in front of me. This one could be it.

An enchanted library that drops exactly the book you need in front of you at the moment you need it? Well that's a king's treatment indeed.

Balastar chuckled in my mind.

Read it to me. Read me whatever you find. I want to hear word for word.

Everything? Yes. Everything.

This is the book of the goddess Awilix and the creation of shadow weaving.

I placed my hand on one of the carvings on the large oak door, then leaned my shoulder and head against it.

He read a line from the first chapter to me.

"Hath before you the twelfth volume of the Master Zol Sen Archives, as a matter of historical record and in establishment of the characteristics of astrological influence on the energetic variances within the conduits of magic in our world."

He continued to scan chapter after chapter of technical Zol Sen accounts of the goddess's history and her desire to remain hidden. The texts explained many things: everything from the physics of the spell being made to the star alignment at the time of the spell to the exact words used by the god and goddess. As Balastar continued to read, I slumped down on the floor and kept listening.

What if we just match up the star alignment and say the spell backwards? Or is that too basic? I asked him.

Yes. That's very basic. That'll never work.

Ok, Ancient One, I defer to you then.

He kept reading. His voice was smooth, deep and soothing. It was hard not to drift off into sleep as he went on reading the more boring parts of the book.

Ok, there's something interesting here.

I blinked a few times and sat upright.

It's a bit hard to understand, but I think I get it.

I chewed my bottom lip. *Let's hear it.*

Balastar seemed to suck in a breath and began:

At the very foundation of every Zol spell is the thread of natural balance of all things in this world and in the cosmos. Hereto, as presented in the Master Zol Sen Archives are the guiding order for all defined energetical shifts in the natural order that influence the magical systems. The rhythms of our year, resulting in seasonal changes, the shortening of days and nights, culminating in the solstices and equinoxes and Fae conduits, in addition to the planetary alignments and cosmic shifts within our solar system and beyond are the source of the magic of our zodiac. Thus, the constructs of zodiac magic will fluctuate and balance must be brought forth by the gods, adapting the natural order through the use of spells to meet the needs of the realms that such gods oversee.

Archive Spell Z-08: In the case of the Spell of Hidden Shadows, the death gods of Xibalba, Vucub-Cane and Hun-Cane, did entreat the binding spell at the sixth equinox. It will be in this channel where one finds the light, that another will only find the dark, where that which has been hidden and protected will need hiding no longer. Just as a new moon cycle sets forth the channel when the sun will rise and a new day begins, so shall Mars retrograde allow an open channel for Awilix to sanction the bond's release.

So, what does that mean? I stood up from the floor and placed my hand on the door again.

This is the Zol Sen way of saying that change is possible. "The sun will rise" represents the desire for the change—or release of the spell—and "the new moon can settle" represents acceptance of the change requested. This means that we can go to Awilix and ask her to grant you your freedom. But expect her to negotiate.

It figures. You have to negotiate everything in Zol Stria. What could we possibly give her in exchange? And where do we find her?

The door creaked open and my eyes flicked to the book he held open in his hands. I watched as the words on the page disappeared. He closed the book carefully and placed it back on the shelf.

"I know where she is. And I know what she wants." He sounded so certain. "We'll present your idea to the war room first, get support from Vucub-Cane and the general. It will require the best people in order to find a goddess that is a master at hiding."

"My unit is the best." There was no mistake about that.

He nodded but didn't say anything as he brushed past me, heading down the hallway and returning to the palace. I kept pace beside him. He better not even think about keeping me out of that war room when he called the meeting. I felt the jaguar within me begin to stir. Lately I'd only shifted during our training exercises, and she was getting restless. She wanted to be set free. It was during times like these, when my mission was clear, that she felt the most restless.

We'll go for a run later, I told her, and with that she began to settle.

CHAPTER 9

The war room was the highest room of the palace. Polished obsidian tile lined the floor, and the ceiling was at least three stories high with detailed carvings and artwork between the beams. Its windows were grand archways with expansive views of the Midnight Gardens and the dark hills and valleys just beyond the molten lake that surrounded the palace. From this height, I could see the pyramids where we'd held the rite and the rows of camps of Dark Zodiac knights that were preparing for the battle for Zol Stria. But no matter how grand the palace was, one could never forget that we were still in the Underworld.

There was a beauty in this grand space that had begun to grow on me. The realm of eternal death and its rulers held its own kind of wonder that was not void of love or joy just because it was dark and far from the view of mortals. This was a more complex system of energy that was no less valuable, no less important, than the world of the light.

I wasn't restless anymore; last night I'd allowed my jaguar form to release in the gardens. We'd run all the way to the lava fields at the edge of the property and circled the grounds one more time after that. It took a lot to calm the beast within me, especially with so much going on.

I heard footsteps and straightened my back, turning around to face the entryway. A warm smile crept over my face as I watched Damian enter. I hurried over to him. "We have a new mission."

"We certainly do," Damian replied. His voice was as cool as usual but his eyes danced with interest.

The rest of my unit began to file in, all of us wearing our battle gear to show our solidarity. That they were allowed entry before everyone meant only one thing: Balastar was honoring me. He'd taken the time to send his messengers to get word to my unit about our plans and ensure they came here first before everyone else.

Bjorn, Andres, Axel, Jenna, Eliana and Lex greeted me with confidence and mission-ready glances. I loved how they were always ready.

I quickly filled them in on what Balastar and I had discovered, our plan for a counterattack and the mission at hand.

"This has never been brought up before, has it? No one's ever tried to break free like this, right?" Eliana asked.

"Nope. We're the first. And we'll be the last. This ends with us," I said.

"I can't believe we're getting our freedom. After all these centuries of nagual being slaves to the gods, I never even considered that we could actually be free of them." Eliana's eyes were bright.

"That's what we're going for, chica," I said.

"If only Zayne were here to see this," Lex said. "For us to even be having this conversation with the generals and Vucub-Cane is a huge step forward."

My chest heaved with love for them. I hoped we would get what we wanted by the end of this meeting.

"The challenge will be convincing Vucub-Cane to release you. The gods' leverage over us gives them unfathomable power. You know all the legends of the great nagual, how they've fought the monsters that cross the Zodiac Gates, preventing the world from falling into the hands of the UnZol creatures that would otherwise torment them. The system of nagual and their shamans upholds the veil. We're the keepers of the Gates. If nagual are no longer bound to the gods, they'll lose one of their greatest assets. Many of those who worship the gods worship them because of the nagual. I'm not sure if Vucub-Cane is willing to give that up," Damian argued.

I pursed my lips. "I'm sure it will be hard, but it can't be impossible. We have to try."

Before I could say anything else, the room became still as we all felt the cold and vast presence of Vucub-Cane. None of us watched him walk in; he simply appeared before us from a mist the colors of ivory and coal. His white hair fell neatly down to his shoulders, his gray eyes lightening as he considered us, his expression cool and thoughtful. He said not a word as he stood there, eyes boring into us.

Next to enter was Balastar, who noted everyone in the room, followed immediately by Solana, his niece. I straightened when Trent appeared. It was the first time I had been in the same room with them since becoming queen, and I felt relieved that my feelings for Trent had finally dissipated. Seeing him just now was freeing in its own way, because I was sure only then that I was no longer in love with him.

Within moments, the room filled with the four generals of the Zol elements, the two Arcana generals and representatives from the Dark Zol legions. Even with all the assembled Fae, the large space with its tall archways gave an even more expansive feeling.

When all had arrived, the grand table in the center of the room immediately came to life with a three-dimensional map of Zol Stria. It was like one of my visions or something from a sci-fi movie where every detail of every part of our world was displayed. I swore I could see minuscule creatures moving around on the landscape, each as small as the tiniest ant.

None of the generals spoke; they stood alert and observing, waiting for the death god to speak first. Again, I noticed that the god's eyes never fell on me and wondered if he even knew why Balastar had called this meeting.

Vucub-Cane placed himself in the center of the room and when he did, whatever mutterings among the assembled Fae were immediately silenced, allowing his every word to bounce sharply and clearly against the walls. "I know you have been meeting regularly with Balastar, and I trust you've formed your strategy well. I was asked to join this meeting just as you were, because your Dark King has an idea to propose that I have not yet agreed to supporting. I am not sure if it will even work. It could either be very smart, or very stupid. Before I decide, I would like you all to hear it for yourselves."

After a beat of silence there were some muttered responses and grunts from the generals. My unit remained still and unwavering; they would support me blindly. Without intending to, my gaze shifted to Trent. Despite our relationship not working out, he was the one person in this room who knew me before I'd become a nagual. It was so strange to think that we were both human once, that we hadn't worried about Fae and monsters. I couldn't help but wonder what was going on in his mind. He seemed stiff, colder than I remembered him. I wondered if I only found him cold because Balastar's blood was warm.

"I appreciate everyone coming together on such short notice." Balastar's voice filled the room with precision and command. Those grumbling voices hushed to silence.

Solana spoke before Balastar could explain anything. "King Balastar."

"Solana," he returned coolly, not expecting to be interrupted.

"Before you begin, I wanted you to be aware of a report from one of our sentinels keeping watch on the wards. This is relevant for all of us here." She stepped forward as if to command attention, but it was already impossible to tear your eyes away from her.

Her silken mass of red hair was tied into a long braid that draped over her shoulder and her dark lashes framed stilling blue eyes.

"Proceed, General," Balastar said.

"Our defenses have been experiencing strange attacks through the wards. The stretch in the fabric between Zol Stria and the Underworld has increased threefold overnight, and the monsters are flooding in with more fury every time. We keep calling in reinforcements and staving them off, but if the stretch keeps increasing at this rate, we will be overwhelmed." As she spoke, the areas where the troops were defending the wards amplified on the large table and we saw what amounted to a live feed of the sentinels defending their positions.

"Also, an hour ago we had two more openings here and here." She pointed to the two gaps in the veil. "Our sentinels are standing by, but nothing has come through yet. I am planning to send my elite force through it to protect it from the other side."

Although I had never seen this calculating and collaborative side of Solana, I figured she must have had it in her to command so much of the mafia on the other side of the Gates. With my love for Trent gone, I almost didn't hate her as much as I had before. I could at least be satisfied with knowing we had her skills on our side and not the other way around.

"Go ahead. Send them through and command your troops to stop killing the Fae and start taking prisoners," Balastar said. "We need to interrogate them and learn more about the armies they are building. Find out anything you can about their attacks."

Solana turned to Trent; he gave a silent nod and left the war room to deploy their orders. I released a silent breath, grateful this whole meeting would be a little less awkward with him gone. Balastar met my gaze with a look that grounded me in an instant.

He turned to face the room. Those around him seemed to shuffle slightly away from him, giving him more space. The death god was the only one in the entire room who'd taken a seat in one of the grand chairs near the window, signaling to us all that Balastar was leading this meeting.

"We have a proposal for a new approach that will allow us to send our most skilled forces, sight unseen, directly into the wolf's den. The most advanced nagual are those that have the ability to shadow weave. Their abilities are amplified by the goddess of the moon's gifts of hidden shadows. This will give us the opportunity to launch a surprise attack on the leaders of Zol Stria. It will be a coup."

There were unfavorable mumblings, grunts and heads shaking among the generals.

A female general spoke up. She had a wild kind of beauty. The elf's face was angular and thin, her eyes stone cold and fierce. I remembered meeting her at dinner a few days ago; her name was Vera. "That is an impossible strategy. The nagual are under the command of the death gods. Hun-Cane will sniff them out the second they make the Climb and take them under his control. In our meeting with you earlier, we all agreed that at this point the nagual should stay down here where they won't be a liability."

I shot a glance at Vucub-Cane, who stiffened slightly.

"How does it work, then?" All eyes darted to me. I'd forgotten that I wasn't just a member of my nagual unit, I was their queen. I straightened and took a deep breath. "If I make the Climb to Zol Stria under Vucub-Cane's control, will Hun-Cane be able to give his own orders and divert us? How does that dynamic actually work?" This had never been an issue before. In the thousands of years of nagual forces, the death gods barely paid any attention to our missions. Now, this simple fact made the difference between winning and losing a war.

Balastar subtly shot me a questioning look. *Where are you going with this?*

I want to know how they see it. I want all the angles before we present our proposal. This way we aren't blindsided.

"Whoever issues the initial command controls the unit and the other brother cannot impose or override orders," Vucub-Cane said from where he sat. "However"—he turned away from the window, his gaze landing on me—"he will know of your exact location at all times. And given that he knows your strengths and weaknesses, he will use them against you to thwart the mission. Which is why we decided not to activate our nagual forces for any attacks outside of the Underworld."

This is exactly what I thought and what I needed established. I sent these thoughts to Balastar. While he feigned indifference, I knew he'd understood me perfectly. In the heartbeats that followed, he didn't speak. He was giving me the space to continue.

"The nagual, and our ability to shadow weave, are the best offensive strategy we have to getting behind enemy lines and taking control of the leaders. When word got out that I, the mate of the UnZol King, am a nagual, many senior nagual joined us and are here in the Underworld awaiting orders from Vucub-Cane. In fact, we all have except for three loyalists, and those three have very strong ties to the Houses of Zol Stria. Yet, the link we have to the death gods is, in fact, our greatest weakness." I scanned the room and tried to read their expressions. They were listening expectantly, and only two generals had dissenting looks on their faces.

"There is a way around this. A way to go in under the radar of Hun-Cane and shadow weave straight to each of the Houses and take out the Vicars without being detected." The dissenters' expressions softened slightly, intrigued. I moved to the front of the room, away from my nagual family, and stood in the empty space next to Balastar. Everyone's eyes fixed on me.

"We must remove the bonds that tie us to the death gods," I declared. "Once we do, we will no longer be under the complete control of those who created us. Instead, we will be following orders because it is our job. Not because Zols are being controlled. The ties between god and nagual will be permanently severed."

"And how do you propose we do that?" Vera, the elven general, said.

"We go to Awilix," I said.

CHAPTER 10

I explained the plan to release the covenant between the gods and the nagual so we could have our free will returned to us. They listened, several generals immediately agreeing and voicing their support of our efforts.

Three generals challenged our strategy. They asked questions to expose flaws in our plan and argued with us at length. They looked to Vucub-Cane for support, for reasons to keep us under his control. He said nothing and remained still and uninvolved.

Balastar defended the plan and wouldn't accept any of their arguments at face value. For every counterpoint raised from the questioning generals, he challenged them by asking something of them. When they suggested we would be challenged by Awilix's shadow beasts, he asked for them to assign us sentinels as reinforcements. When they said she would find this tiresome and not worth her time, he asked them to send at least four of the most senior nagual with us to show support from even the oldest among us.

When they suggested that the spell was old and Awilix would find it a nuisance and a waste of energy, Balastar asked them to assign two of their Master Zol Shamans to accelerate the channeling of cosmic energy. He asked them to design special elixirs to assist with healing, travel, strength and insight.

I honestly didn't know at what point in time he'd done it, but he had considered just about every possible obstacle we would face in order to achieve this mission. He already had a list of requests for each general that tapped into their unique strengths and resources.

With this kind of planning, it was no wonder he had won so many of his past battles. He must have believed in the plan to have applied so much thought to it. It seemed his brain was working at a much faster pace than my own. The heat that raised within me everytime I was around him, rose once again to the surface like a glowing ember in a kindling fire. He had come through, in a big way, and I wouldn't forget it.

After several rounds of challenges and demands, one of the dissenting generals spoke up. He was General Nokovic of the Zol Wolves and his forces were the largest of all the armies in our ranks.

"And why would Awilix even bother to release the bond? She's not known for helping anyone out of the kindness of her heart." The general chuckled, and the two other generals challenging us grunted and scoffed in agreement.

"Because we have something she wants. Something she's always wanted. And now is the time we return it to her," Balastar said. He hadn't shared this with me at all and even though I hated being surprised by a detail like this, I was eager to hear what it was Awilix wanted. I'd have to talk to him about his communication skills later.

"Ah, Balastar. You clever bastard," the white-haired general said. He'd been introduced to me as General Clastinze the other day. All I knew was I didn't like the way he gaze always lingered a little too long. I got the icky feeling he was undressing me in his mind. His had the look of a man who took what he wanted, and if he tried that shit with me, I'd have to school him real quick

"Please, do share with the group," Vera insisted, her square jaw tight.

"When the Gates closed the veil between the mortal lands and Zol Stria, it focused most of Awilix's magic right into Zol Stria. Some of her magical moon energy does affect the human world, but not nearly as much as it would if the channels were open," explained Balastar.

This was common information, taught in all the Academies of Zol Stria.

"Which is why so many humans can't tap into their intuition and sixth sense as much," I added.

"Exactly," Balastar said. "When we win the war against Zol Stria, we will be opening the Gates and allowing the worlds of Fae and mortal to meet. We will finally combine our worlds, as we have always wanted. The Zol Sen have wanted this for us for centuries, since I was a young boy they have prophesized that bringing our worlds together is the natural order. But we must do it carefully. Calculated and controlled. For our worlds to join, mortals will need to feel the strength of the moon's energy to have access to some level of magic so they can coexist with Fae. Our first measure of control is to only allow those Fae who receive clearance to enter the human world and begin to slowly educate them on our kind. We will work in partnership with the Zodiac General Command, those military commanders and world leaders of the mortal lands who already know of our presence. Solana has made excellent progress in these talks and, for the most part, they see the benefits of merging our worlds."

The table changed images to show us the future vision for both our worlds. In this rendering, the Zodiac Gates were open, allowing Fae to enter the human lands and humans to cross over to Zol Stria. I had to admit, it moved me that he had already put so much effort into preparing this elaborate presentation.

"Awilix has been suppressed all these thousands of years, unable to experience the full extent of her power," Balastar said. "Those who have encountered her have told us she came across as restrained and depressed. This is because Zol Stria's rule under the Zol Council has thrown the magic systems of our world out of balance. By releasing the bond between the nagual and the death gods, she will be the catalyst that helps restore balance in our world. The moon's energy will flow freely in Zol Stria once again. Once we meet with her, she will see the value in our efforts and will want to support us, I'm sure of it." Balastar had indeed thought of everything.

"Fellow Zol Generals, let's take a moment for deliberation," General Clastinze said.

Balastar looked over at Vucub-Cane, who nodded slightly. "Fine idea. We'll reconvene after some refreshments in the hall," Balastar said.

We filed out of the room, leaving the three opposing generals to their discussions. Vucub-Cane remained in the war room with them as the rest of us left.

When we returned after our break, I scanned the generals' faces. They were relaxed but unreadable. Once we were all present, Vera stepped forward. Her eyes fixed on Balastar.

"Although I wasn't around when you first ruled," she began, "I have studied your war strategies and always considered them somewhat elaborate, yet extremely precise. You never made a move without anticipating three to four potential outcomes. I always considered it a shame that you never fully achieved your goal for the Dark Zodiac all those years ago.

"As you know, after your capture, we fell to the forces of Zol Stria and have been under their oppression for all these years. Although many of us have tried to resume the fight, we never could unite our people the way you did. I believe that if you had not been captured, our world would have taken a completely different course and the bonds of slavery and oppression would not have plagued our people for so long. Yet I do not follow you blindly. None of us do." She motioned to the other generals flanking her.

"There is a lot at stake, for all of us." Now she addressed the room. Her eyes scanned those of the other generals. "There are many lives on the line and we must evaluate every possibility before following you to war. We have our own needs to be met, and before we agree to the plan, you must agree to our terms."

"And what are your terms?" Balastar said with no hesitation. I wondered if he had already considered this, too.

"That you name a successor and put in place a hierarchy to rule if you are ever again captured. We cannot afford to go another thousand years without a ruler in your place."

"Then your queen, my mate, is my successor, and we will work on having an heir to the throne soon." Balastar didn't look at me and I was grateful, because I could feel my cheeks begin to heat. We hadn't even consummated our marriage, and I wasn't ready to.

I'm about to go into battle and they want me to try and make a baby? Seriously?

Balastar still didn't look at me, but he responded, *It's the way of the Fae to sire heirs. We'll talk about this later.*

I look forward to it.

I almost caught mirth in his eyes as he sent me his thoughts, and my center began to warm with a silent giggle.

Vera looked as though she was going to ask something else when Balastar spoke again. "And should anything happen to me, or my queen, before our child is born, we will name a successor."

The generals were silent and I took that as an agreement.

"Now that this is settled, we agree to the strategy of freeing the nagual forces. It's solid." Vera's voice was icy and direct, but her shoulders had relaxed and her jaw wasn't nearly as tightly clenched as it had been just moments ago. In fact, the thick wall of tension in the room seemed to dissipate all together.

"And so do I," Vucub-Cane finally spoke, his voice filling the room and commanding all attention. The death god must have subdued his presence before, because now it was impossible not to be overwhelmed by the vast and utter power he imposed on us.

Balastar and I exchanged glances; he gave me a slight nod. I couldn't help but plaster a great big smile on my face at what we had achieved. Jenna, who was standing just behind me, placed a hand on my shoulder. Bjorn nudged me slightly and I couldn't wait to turn around and hug them all. This was a huge win for all of us, for all nagual ever born and those to come. As long as we completed the mission, that was.

"Drinks on me," Bjorn whispered out of the side of his mouth as the generals filed out of the room.

"This is it," Andres said, clearly relieved. "We're going to be free."

I lifted my chin and said, "Yes! And it's about fucking time."

CHAPTER 11

All the generals left for the evening, and Balastar, Damian and I remained in the war room to go over the strategy to get to Awilix.

"I still don't see why this needs to be so difficult," I said. "Why can't we just call her? Or send an owl with a letter. Why do we have to trek through those impossible mountains, then shadow weave into her closed-off caves, then search for her in the dark? It seems like this could be so much easier than what you're suggesting."

"Because she is a goddess. A goddess does not come to you. You go to her," Balastar replied.

"Exactly. And Awilix doesn't like to be bothered. She's not known for being a friendly goddess," Damian added.

"So run this by me one more time," I said, forcing my eyes to stay fixed on the three-dimensional map on the war room table. I found it was becoming an effort to take my attention off Balastar, his presence all-consuming. I wasn't just attracted to him by the mate bond, even though that was for sure happening. I had just gotten better at supressing those desires that rose in me. But now I was starting to respect him on an intellectual level.

He walked us through the mission again and I asked multiple questions on the approach, but all his answers were solid.

Soon after, Damian excused himself to go and do whatever it was Damian did on his free time. I had a pretty good idea that he was going to find the elf general Vera and make his move. He certainly liked to keep his bed warm. There'd been Ixia, Gaelle, the Fae bartender back at the Academy... I had lost track of all the others.

I made to leave soon after when Balastar reached for my wrist. I could count on one hand the amount of physical contact we'd had since his revival.

Startled, I turned to face him. I'd been focused on the mission and on how to execute it until his eyes locked with mine and I almost forgot my own fucking name. There was no doubt that Balastar's face was far beyond the most handsome I had ever seen, but he was still a huge mystery. And it was just now, as he pinned me with his gaze, that I didn't care.

"Before you go, I'd like to talk to you," he said softly and my eyes lingered on his soft lips. They were full, smooth and perfectly balanced on his face.

Although he still held my wrist in his hand, he wasn't demanding. In fact, the look on his face told me he hoped I would say yes. My body wanted me to say yes. It wanted to stay and listen to whatever this gorgeous man had to say, and there was that strange, confused part of me that was hoping he would do a whole lot more than just talk. My body wanted him to *do* things. I held my breath and shoved those thoughts down real quick. *Focus.*

"Actually, I've got to go. It's late and I'll be up early tomorrow to train with Bjorn." When I pulled my hand from his grip, he let my wrist slip out. I took a step away. It wasn't the direction my body wanted me to go, but my logical brain decided I had to put some distance between us.

"You don't need to be afraid of me," he said.

"I'm not afraid of you." I no longer saw him as the villain in all of this, like the Zol Council set him up to be. But at this point, the thing I was afraid of was how I felt when I was around him. How I fantasized about him at night and couldn't stop fixing my eyes on his lips. I wanted to step back again, but I held myself in place as if standing still could prove I wasn't afraid.

"Your eyes say differently. So does the way your heart beats when I'm around you. It's much faster, giving you away." His eyes flashed in amusement.

In Zol Stria, a Fae's aura was our emotional giveaway. We learned how to retract our auras in order to hide what we were feeling from others, because showing emotion was the fastest way to get yourself killed or become someone's bitch. So we went about our days with retracted auras and deflector spells lifted around us to keep our emotions and conversations hidden. But I couldn't hide my heartbeat. Only certain beasts like the hunting nagas of Aries Gate, vampires, or those of vampire species like the Craven of Libra, could hear the heartbeats of others. It made me wonder, what was he exactly?

"I'm sure there are lots of reasons that my heart beats fast, and it has nothing to do with you," I said.

He closed the gap between us. My throat hitched the moment he stood before me, his height making me feel small. Instantly his fine, musky scent slid along my skin and intoxicated my senses.

"Are you sure about that?" He trailed a finger down my arm.

I shuddered and tried to raise a deflector spell, but something seemed to be blocking my power.

"You don't have to hide yourself from me. In fact, I think it would be better if you didn't." His look was downright predatory.

I squeezed my thighs together to control the heat rising in my core. "Why shouldn't I hide myself? I barely know you. And by the way, are you somehow blocking my deflector spell?" I was shocked at how calm my voice sounded.

He chuckled slightly. "No, cariño. You can't raise a deflector spell in front of your mate. I can't raise one either. The magic of the zodiac made it this way, I'm guessing so we would have honest conversations, and not hide anything from each other." He cocked his head to one side and I caught sight of a tattoo that curled up around his neck. I wanted to reach my hand out and touch it, but I held myself back.

"You make it sound like we're in some kind of real relationship, but the truth is I just met you. I—" Before I could speak another word, his mouth was on mine. I reached my hands up to his chest to push him back, but our contact sparked something. A rush of emotion flooded into me, longing being the strongest one of all. It was as though all these years, hidden deeply in my soul, was an unsatisfied ache for his touch.

He kissed me urgently, longing for me as much as I ached for him. He kissed me exactly how I needed to be kissed in that moment. Like he demanded me. Demanded I respond to him. Demanded I remember who he was to me and who we were together. It was as though that deep, unknown part of me suddenly woke up and realized who I'd always been.

My back arched and I leaned into him, wrapping my arms around his neck as he swept his hands along my waist. There was a tightness in his touch. A huge part of me wanted him to just rip right through my clothes and throw me on the table. As much as it pained me, I pulled myself back and took a breath.

"Why does this feel so right?" My whole body shook at the realization. It was as though a door had opened to my closed-off, battered heart and he was walking right in. I couldn't just let him, could I? He only wanted me for the power I gave him. Not because he truly loved me.

"There goes your heartbeat again." He reached up and placed his hand on my chest where my heart was, his touch igniting my skin. "You're thinking too much."

I nodded. He was right. I didn't have to be afraid of him. At least, not right now. I could just give into the lust of the moment, couldn't I? I could give in to the desire I had pooling from the depths of me. My shoulders relaxed.

"This is not the story of the Dark Fae uprising." His eyes bored into mine. "This is not at all about the rebellion's fight against Zol Stria."

"It's not?" I tilted my head to the side, and he lifted his hand to my jaw.

"No. This is our story. Me and you, and everything we can do together." The sensuality with which he said those words warmed me to my core.

You know what, sometimes you have to say fuck it.

Oh really?

Shit, I thought I said that to myself.

I'm glad you didn't.

CHAPTER 12

H is lips met mine, and this time I didn't pull back. I pressed myself against him. I wanted to feel all of him on me, around me, inside me. He scooped me in his arms and I entwined shadow mist around us both, covering us completely in a tumbling dark cloud. With my arms around his neck, I pulled my lips away from his and said, "Let's get out of here."

"Yes, please do the honors," he said.

I gave him a sly smile before shadow weaving us to my room. While he held me in the darkness, I took in his scent, my hands ever-conscious of the way his firm muscles felt during our contact. My heart beat faster as I grew more excited. As soon as we arrived, I used my fire element to light a few candles, just enough for the yellow-and-orange flames to glow against the walls.

His lips curled into a smile and I smiled back. Every time I was around him, I was on the brink of caving and giving in to the pull of his energy. The longing he brought up in me was absolutely suffocating. Now that I was in his arms, I could sense that I'd always been pulled to him. Like the gravity of a planet and its moon. Our magic connected, merged, and electrified my senses.

He slid me slowly down his body and began to help me out of my battle gear, and I helped him remove his shirt. Every movement was slow; he wasn't rushing this. My breath came in heavy pants at the sight of him. Even in the low light I could see every curve of his shoulders, stomach and chest. His muscular frame was so much more than I even imagined, making me crave him more by the second. And when I helped him unbuckle his pants, the size of his cock made my breath catch. It was huge. Perfect, smooth, beautiful and just, *huge*.

Soon his lips were on mine again, then on my neck, then down my chest as his hands reached for me eagerly. While I writhed with pleasure from his gripping caresses, I wondered if he would even fit inside me. Now I had a different reason to be afraid, only this reason aroused me.

"I've been practicing so much restraint these past few days. There are so many things I've wanted to do to you since I saw you again," he growled. "Because you are, and have always been, mine."

My heart pounded in my chest. Before I could respond, he lifted me in his arms again and this time my legs curled around his waist. He set me down on the thick, dark-burgundy comforter of the king-sized bed.

He reached for me, his hands exploring my every curve and teasing their way down to the warmth of my center. I grew even warmer as heat pooled between my legs, a torrent of desire coursing through me. The taste of him as my mouth felt his tongue dance against mine stoked the fire in me. The roaring need for him made me lose some of my sanity as a deeper, hidden feeling of having been denied him threatened to surface with every kiss. I savored every touch and sought him out. Grasping at him, welcoming this moment instead.

His fingers were soon inside my folds, making me clench and moan. I ached for more and ground myself against him. His tongue traced down to my chest, then my breast was in his mouth. He went to one, then the other, as I grew wetter. My pulse raced faster. I needed more of him.

"All of you..." I moaned. "I need all of you."

"I came back from the Void... for you," he growled. The scrape of his tongue against my chest raised goose bumps on my neck. His kisses worked their way down, dragging heat in their wake until his tongue was between my thighs. He gave me a dark smile before stealing the breath from my throat when his tongue met my center, rolling and satiating my impulses until I screamed in release. It was all I needed to drive me absolutely insane with the need for him to be inside me.

He met my longing by crashing himself into me. I screamed from the pain of the pressure, pressure that turned to a succulent sort of stinging.

He tried again, this time slower, until I opened up enough for him to enter a few centimeters at a time. I moaned with that painful kind of pleasure with each thrust. I responded to his every force with my own. When he was almost entirely inside me, energy and power coursed through my body in a way I had never felt before. It was as though I could feed off his energy, just like I fed off dark energy.

"I feel something. I feel your power," I moaned.

"And I feel yours."

As strong and powerful as he was, he knew exactly what I wanted. Without a word, he lay on his back and let me climb on top of him. His powerful chest heaved as his eyes took me in. The delicious strength in having the UnZol King between my legs and in my control was more than I could have imagined. Unrelenting power threaded through me as I lowered myself onto him and began to thrust.

Sweat formed on my brow as I gave him all of me. I felt him deep within and he fed me his energy, filling me up with all of him.

We explored each other frantically, desperately. In his every caress, I found a part of myself that I was missing. Every passionate touch woke another hidden piece of myself. I groaned as he returned my desire harder and faster each time until I was gasping for breath. It was more than I could bear as the pleasure inside me reached an absolute peak and he met me there at the same time. I had fallen prey to my desire for him, and I wasn't the least bit sorry.

I collapsed to his side, completely out of breath as my muscles relaxed. I shut my eyes for a moment, relishing the sweet release of the dark energy that was no longer blocked within me. I could feel my shadows growing, expanding and touching every part of this room.

I turned my head and looked over at him. His eyes were closed as though in a silent meditation. I placed my hand on the ribbed muscles of his chest, not wanting the intimacy of our connection to have been an illusion. He placed his hand on top of mine and looked at me.

My shadows curled around him familiarly, protectively. My darkness had hidden him all those years ago, and it all flooded back to me. Wisps of my dark mist instinctively coiled around us as we lay here. I let the mist lead me to those memories and I allowed them in.

I saw myself in his arms much like we were now, only not in this Underworld palace but in our own castle. I floated around inside this memory and watched. There were many years of our relationship that had nothing to do with war. There were strolls in parks and watching theater performances. There were candlelight dinners and mountain hikes. There was a real relationship that grew naturally and true. My heart felt fuller as I watched us together. It was more than I had imagined.

The memory faded, bringing me back to this moment we now shared. He reached to run a hand through my hair. His hand fell gently on my shoulder, as though he was also making sure I was really there with him

"Is this real?" I asked.

"Yes, it's real. And now you don't have to play hard to get anymore. You remember how we were together, don't you?" His gentle touch made my heart melt.

"Some part of me awoke just now. I can't explain it exactly, but I remember this feeling. Being with you felt like finding another part of myself that I forgot existed. And I feel more power. Like my shadows and fire element are somehow stronger." I looked at my hands as though the magic of our connection would reveal itself there.

"We just consummated our mating. Our energy is now one. I feed off your power, you feed off mine, and between the both of us, nothing can stop us." He considered me. "It was driving me crazy that you were so close but I couldn't have you." He turned on his side, eyes intent and awake. "I couldn't stand it when you didn't remember me. It took every bit of self-control I had not to grab you and make you remember who you were back then. But, I'm glad I didn't. You came to me willingly, and now, you're mine. And there is no end to what we can be together."

I swallowed down any remaining hesitations I may have had left of him, of us and of what this all meant. No matter how much I fought it, there was a primordial connection between us that I just couldn't deny.

"The stars write the path," I said. "Who am I to question fate?"

"True. The stars write the path," he said sleepily.

"Balastar?"

"Yes."

"We forgot to raise a contraceptive spell," I said.

"We can't. There must be an heir," he said lightly.

"Oh shit, that's right." I fidgeted. It took Fae lots and lots of tries to get pregnant. Rarely did a Fae get pregnant on the first try. I remembered the students at the Academy telling me how their siblings had twenty to thirty-year age differences, which wasn't that big of a deal when you lived hundreds of years, but considering I came from the mortal realm, it sounded like a really long time. I breathed a sigh of relief when I thought of it that way. I wasn't ready for kids.

He smiled with hooded eyes and then shut them softly. I watched him breathe until the dark blanket of sleep covered me.

CHAPTER 13

DAMIAN

They say patience is a virtue. I say it's just a matter of time before the stars find a way to close the karmic circle.

Vera, the beautiful elven general I had the pleasure of meeting recently, was sleeping in my bed with the sheets curled around her. It was late as I sat in a chair in my room admiring her bare legs. Her every curve was perfection, her taste as sweet as a Zol Rose, and her center as hot as molten lava.

I enjoyed watching her after our hours of friction in those very sheets. It wasn't lost on me that her people would be pissed if they knew she was here. The magical elves of Libra were rarely seen outside their territory. They had strict rules about being around other Fae and so kept themselves secluded to their lands. They said it was because they were the purest conduits for zodiac magic, that only their magic was strong enough to keep the balance of nature. Some said their beliefs were from the old ways and arrogant, and I was inclined to agree.

And it was that kind of arrogance that got the elves exploited by the Vicars for their own wealth and control. Their exploitation by the Zol Council raised the stakes for the elves, but the truth was that every one of us had a big stake in all of this.

I had abandoned my role as a shaman of Zol Stria all those years ago because of the death of Lily, Sasha's aunt. But when I'd left it wasn't like I hadn't seen the corruption in Zol Stria. It wasn't like that hadn't bother me. In fact, I hadn't liked a lot of what I saw, but their marginalization didn't affect me. I was untouchable as a shaman for the death gods.

I'd been wrapped up in myself back then. I hadn't cared what had happened to Sasha, or anyone else, when I left. I'd just wanted to get away from the bullshit system and think about something other than Lily and the pain I felt.

Then I became a completely different person. By some twist of fate, I found solace in being there for Sasha. She grew on me. Like a niece grew on an uncle, I guess. Being there for her was what Lily would've wanted. Realizing that, I'd decided to help her, for Lily. But that wasn't why I was here for her now. I was here now because I wanted to be.

I turned my attention to the window as a squad of Arcana Angels flew overhead. They were on twenty-four-hour watch shifts. Their wide, black wings were barely visible against the black cave ceiling miles above us. Beyond the palace were the military camps, and farther beyond those was the veil with tears in it that was being defended by our forces. As the generals formed their plans to overtake Zol Stria, I'd been planning my revenge on Ixia.

Ever since I'd learned Zol Stria had taken her back among their ranks, I knew exactly which side I was on. It was a no-brainer. A few days ago I formed an alliance with Carly so I could access her resources and enlist the help of the Zolari Trolls that mined the caves. They had an intricate tunnel system and were left very much unchecked by the death gods. Thousands of years of servitude had left them unquestionably loyal. Supposedly.

Zolari Trolls could Climb in and out of the Underworld through hidden entrances known only to them. That had been news to me. In fact, I was sure none other than the trolls themselves knew of these passageways. Zol Stria viewed them as savage creatures that were not to be crossed, so why go out of your way to talk to one of them?

Legend had it that they lived under bridges, scaring off travelers with a single look and turning those who threatened them to stone. When anyone went to look for them, they vanished. Until I saw them in the death gods' gardens, I'd thought the trolls were a myth.

The trolls didn't want anyone coming into their caves. The idea that their hidden homes would be at risk was reason enough for them to stand with us. So, Carly helped me begin talks with the Zolari Troll elders so that I could use their tunnel system to reach Aquarius Gate and get to Ixia.

Vera shifted in the bed. This was starting to feel like the quiet before the storm, and I had better make the most of it. I made my way back to her and ran my hands along her exposed thigh. She responded with a sensual rounding of her hips and a soft sigh. I reached my hand around her, caressing her stomach then tracing my fingers along her belly button. She responded to my touch with a low moan. I dragged my hand down along her abdomen and reached her center, rubbing softly first, then circling it with more pressure. She was already warm. Already wet.

"Sorry to wake you up, but I couldn't help myself," I admitted, but I wasn't sorry.

"Actually, I think I was just dreaming about you," she whispered as I kissed her neck. That was all I needed to hear. It was time to go another round.

◈

As soon as the sun came up, I headed to Carly's quarters and banged on her door. She gave me a single nod when she opened it and swiftly came with me, closing the door behind her. We walked down the hall with purpose, then down the main stairs, through the kitchen and out the back door. The tiny suns cast a golden light across the black-and-gray flora, making it seem as though it was catching fire.

"Carly, wait," I said, hoping she would stop walking so fast. She stopped and turned, her lips pressed together in annoyance.

"Let's go over this one more time," I said.

"No. We are not going over this again." Her eyes darted around us suspiciously. "Now keep up or I'm going without you." Even with the deflector spell up, she felt the need to whisper.

"I think you're letting your recent promotion to Master Shaman get to your head," I grunted. She was so damn bossy but I guessed it came with the territory. While my lack of interest in playing politics had kept me from being promoted to Master Shaman, Carly had used her interest in them to seize the advantage of the impending war and take that position for herself.

We walked for a while in the woods, following a worn trail that led to a large boulder. Carly placed her hand on it and whispered an incantation. The boulder's rough surface dissipated before us, leaving a rocky archway in its place. The smell inside was woody and damp. Sconces of firelight lined the large chamber within, and there, sitting on the ground, were the three Zolari Troll elders. We stepped inside.

Carly reached inside her black shaman's cloak for a small bag of golden Zol Coin, which were the currency of Zol Stria. The eldest Zolari Troll outstretched a bark-like arm and opened her palm. Carly placed a single golden coin and bowed, repeating the gesture for all three elders. This was more than the exchange of money; it was a show of goodwill and respect for the elders' time and safe passage.

Behind us, the boulder that had crumbled away began to build itself back up. A tall, lean figure dressed in black battle gear tumbled in among the rubble just before the boulder could complete its reformation. The intruder crouched there, kneeling on one knee with her knuckles against the ground. Blonde-streaked hair flew in wisps around her head as she kept her eyes cast down.

"Forgive my trespass," she said. "The stars wrote this path for me. I must join you on your mission to infiltrate the Great Houses of Zol Stria." She slowly lifted her gaze to meet mine.

"Vera," I breathed in disbelief. "You shouldn't have come. You have your army to lead. This is a very risky mission." I hadn't known Vera long but I respected her immensely. She was tough as nails. She pushed back. She fought for her people. All the while being wildly attractive and sensual. I didn't want to be responsible for anything bad happening to her.

The elders stirred, exchanging glances and whispering to one another.

"We only agreed to grant passage to two travelers. Not three. We will not allow it," said an elder with wide black eyes in raspy Spanish.

Vera stood from her crouched position and walked over to Carly. "My sister is being held by House Aquarius. She and her family are bound to them, never allowed to leave. They feed off her magic and have taken her children. She has been suffering too long. Please, let me put an end to this. I will be forever in your debt." Her eyes of clear-blue crystal penetrated Carly's as Vera held her hands out in front of her, her stare a mixture of rage and grief.

Carly shifted uncomfortably. "First of all, your following us and interrupting our meeting is entirely unacceptable." She huffed and released an incantation that sounded harsh in ancient Mayan. "How did you even know we were coming here? How long have you been spying on us? Following us? Who else knows you're here? And don't you even consider lying to me. One of the areas where I excelled in my studies was casting truth spells. If you lie to me, your tongue will turn to stone in your mouth."

Vera didn't break her stance, her feet planted in place and her gaze locked on Carly. "I overheard Sasha talking to Damian about Ixia being at House Aquarius. Everyone knows how she betrayed him." Vera turned to look at me now. "When you left the room this morning, I had no idea where you were going, or what you were doing, but I followed you in the hopes that it would lead me to Aquarius. I have spoken to no one about my plans. No one else knows I'm here, I swear it." Her eyes darted back to Carly.

Carly chanted the spell, "*Xen il echan.*" Then she said, "She speaks the truth."

I took a step toward Vera. "This will be dangerous. I can't let you do this." The decades of my torment over Lily's death still lingered in my soul. I clenched my fists and hesitated before saying the next few words, but they had to be said. "You are the first woman I've had any feelings for in a very long time. I can't stand the idea of anything happening to you in Zol Stria. Especially not because of me."

She'd smiled briefly when I'd admitting having feelings for her, but now her face deadpanned. "I'm sorry for what happened to Lily. I truly am. But I am not her and I am not your responsibility. This is my decision, not yours."

I blinked a few times and shook my head. "Fine. You're obviously not going to listen to me, but I still can't let you go in my place." There was too much at stake for me. "On the other hand, if Carly will allow it, you can go in her place." I placed a hand on my chest. "I will be honored to have an elven general at my side."

Carly turned her attention to the elders who were engaged in some sort of interaction of their own, seemingly unconcerned with our affairs. She brought her hand to her brow and rubbed her forehead, considering it.

Damian continued, "After all, Carly, you're a valuable asset to the UnZol King and his queen because of your position as the death god's chosen shaman. You are much needed at their side as they prepare for battle."

"Fine." She gritted out between her teeth. "Damian's right. I was nervous about leaving my post anyway. There are many shamans on our side, but they have no leader if both Damian and I leave. I'll stay and you will go. However, for the record, I am not at all pleased with how you went about this." Carly tsked.

Vera reached for Carly's hands and bowed her head deeply in gratitude. Her emotions wafted over me, her aura glowing purple and white so Carly could feel how much this meant to her.

"Thank you," Vera said, tears spilling over with relief.

Carly approached the elders, explained the exchange and bid them farewell. Soon I would be making the Climb with Zolari Troll magic and now Vera was coming.

Even though it made me nervous to think of what could possibly go wrong, I was glad to have a warrior like Vera by my side.

CHAPTER 14

It was beyond freezing in the Underworld the moment Awilix arrived at the death god's palace. The armies huddled together around fires in the blistering cold. They had put on every layer of clothing they owned and it still wasn't enough. The UnZol King commanded that the fire elements light every chimney and set up bonfires every few yards.

Before we made the trip to visit the goddess, Balastar asked Vucub-Cane to see if she would come here. To all our surprise she'd agreed. It'd saved us the seemingly impossible trip through the Shadow Lands, but no one told us that her very presence would bring about a bone-chilling cold that could freeze your blood in minutes.

"Someone needs to tell Vucub-Cane that he should have warned us about the cold. This could kill some of our soldiers and make many very ill. It will put us at a severe disadvantage." My teeth were shaking as I spoke, my breath turning to icy frost the moment it left my throat. I paced the war room anxiously.

"I will speak to him." Balastar rubbed his hands together and blew on them.

"I've asked the kitchen to prepare hot soup but it freezes the moment it leaves the stove. We're handing out blankets and burning any wood available. The air elements are keeping the air circulating but this is all quite an effort. Can we meet with Awilix already? The quicker we meet the faster she can leave and we can get our warm weather back." My face had gotten so cold it was numb and I was afraid I would begin losing extremities any moment.

Just then, Bat Eyes entered the war room.

"The death god and the goddess will meet with you now," he said with his head bowed. His lips were blue, and for the briefest of moments, I didn't hate him. Actually, I was worried he was on the brink of hypothermia.

"Great. Let's go." I darted down the hall, Balastar keeping pace next to me.

Two more Arcana Angels flanked the door to the death god's private conference room. One of the angels bowed his head slightly and entered the room to announce our arrival. The doors opened wide to receive us just a few short heartbeats later.

There were no images or photos of the moon goddess. She was rarely ever seen except for in old paintings where she was elegantly flying through the air in a cloud of shadows. Little detail was offered and her presence was left up to the imagination. So, I didn't know what to expect. When I saw her, I couldn't take my eyes off her. She seemed to glow like the light of the moon, which was a stark contrast to the shadows that clung to her like a long, black chiffon scarf. They curled around her glossy midnight hair, olive arms and shoulders. I was swept away by her beauty, at once both calm and chilling.

There was only silence as I looked upon the death god and moon goddess sitting at the conference room. Their vast and immeasurable power wafted over us, sucking all the air out of the room and commanding the attention of everyone around them. I couldn't place the strangeness I felt coming from their eyes. It was as if they were aliens, entirely detached and disconnected from our reality.

In my awe of the sheer power present in the room, I couldn't find words. I released a breath when Balastar finally spoke, saving me from fumbling out something stupid.

"Your Grace, you honor us with your presence." Balastar bowed with his hands formed in prayer before him, and I followed suit.

She stared at him blankly, and I took in her smoky black eyes and equally black hair. A single streak of bright white mingled with the thick waves that fell around her shoulders.

"I have little interest in your worldly concerns, so please, let's get on with this." Her melodic voice echoed off the walls. All the while, it was an effort to keep my teeth from chattering.

"Before we begin, why is it so fucking cold?" I'd tried to suppress my frustration, but it was just so damn cold.

"Is it?" She examined her nails.

"Your Grace," Balastar interjected quickly, "would you be so kind as to lift the cold so our soldiers don't freeze before the battle?"

The death god Vucub-Cane raised an elegant white eyebrow and looked to the moon goddess. He must have been immune to the cold because he showed no signs of discomfort. "Awilix, it would help our war effort if you showed the Dark Zodiac your warmer side."

"And why do I care about helping with the war effort? I create balance in this world, I don't take sides."

The room became colder by the second. Ice began to form on the walls and crackle in a thin layer on the floor. "Please," I managed to say as the cold gripped my throat. "We will all die if it gets any colder."

"Fine." She flicked her wrist and the temperature began to rise. The ice that had formed on the walls began to melt. Within moments I could feel my fingers and toes again.

As my body began to feel somewhat normal, I thanked the stars that Balastar had expected her to be difficult. In fact, he'd planned on it by setting up those bonfires in camp just before she'd arrived.

"Now, that's wonderful. Thank you, Your Grace," Balastar said. Just then, cheers and laughter could be heard coming from the outside. "It seems the army shares my sentiment."

If the moon goddess and the death god were moved by the people's cheers, they certainly hid it well.

"Now then, let's get on with it. Why have you called me here?" Awilix said, boredom lacing her words.

"We would like you to release the bond between the death gods and the nagual," I blurted out. A shiver ran down my spine at the icy glare she gave me.

"I arrive at your invitation, Vucub-Cane, and all I get are demands from your people," Awilix told the death god, her face as frosty as the floor had just been.

Balastar had warned me not to speak to him through the bond while we met with the gods. He'd explained that although the gods couldn't understand every word we said to each other, they could sense the vibrations of any communication between us and he didn't want them to think we were holding anything back. But I was dying to tell him what I really thought of this moon goddess. That piece of information wouldn't have been helpful, though, so I guess it was a good thing I couldn't say anything.

"Vucub-Cane, whatever do they mean?" She looked to the death god as if we were babbling children.

Vucub-Cane leaned in slightly, his face void of expression. I still thought I saw amusement alive in his eyes. "You know, the spell that bound the nagual to me and my brother?"

Awilix returned a blank stare.

"This was during the Celestial Creation, when the shamans needed protection to travel between the Fae realm and Earth," he reminded her. "But that outdated system has run its course. We no longer have need of the nagual and would like to free ourselves of the burden of this attachment." Vucub-Cane had made it sound as if we were inconsequential. But the truth of it was that whatever he needed to tell her was fine with me, as long as she agreed to lift the spell.

"Oh, yes. It's coming back to me now." Slowly, she tilted her head to one side, considering me. "Binding spells like that draw from the same gravitational pull that the planets have with their moons. Am I to assume you will want the nagual that are alive now to continue living?" She looked me up and down as though I was, again, inconsequential.

I swallowed down my building rage to scream, "Of course I do," and nodded instead.

"Then there will need to be a sacrifice. An exchange, if you will, so as not to throw the magic off balance and kill you and your fellow nagual," she said.

My mind raced. "What do we have to give in exchange?"

"I was just getting to that part." Awilix leaned back in her chair. "*You* will do just fine. You must transit the Moon Ward in exchange for your freedom. This is no small ask, mind you."

I could have sworn Vucub-Cane's eyes opened wide for the briefest moment, revealing a hint of uncharacteristic surprise. My eyes darted to Balastar, who cleared his throat as a protective tightening gripped me through the bond between us.

"I'll do whatever it takes," I said.

Sasha, you don't know what you're saying. No one's ever gone through the Moon Ward with her and returned.

Then I guess I'll be the first.

CHAPTER 15

DAMIAN

We walked for miles down long, damp passageways. Smaller tunnels lined the sides of the main cave. They were carved from stone and dirt and led to where the Zolari Troll tribes lived, or so I imagined. Dim lights emitted from deep in the tunnels and footsteps could be heard scurrying from the inside.

As we walked, round eyes peered at us from behind corners. The Zolari Troll children were naturally curious but shy.

I felt sweat forming on my brow and my legs became heavy. I wanted to stop, but the elders never needed to stop and it didn't seem Vera did, either, so I just kept going at their pace.

Finally, after a full day of traveling these caves, the trail we were on began to go up. It was like walking straight up the side of a mountain, and when we reached the top, we came across a large dead end with nothing but rock and sediment.

The three elders placed their hands on a rock at the far end of the alcove at the same time, but the rock didn't dissipate as it had inside the Underworld. Instead, it looked entirely the same.

"You, go through now," said the tallest elder. His voice was worn and scratchy.

Vera and I exchanged glances and took several steps forward, pausing before what appeared to be a solid boulder the color of coal.

"What's on the other side?" I asked.

"Aquarius forest. No one will see you. You go two miles north. Then you see town," said the troll.

"And can we come back in this way?"

"You wait. Not fast. Very slow. Place hand on boulder." The troll demonstrated for us. "Then we come for you."

"Vamonos," I said, flashing Vera a smile.

"Vamonos," she replied, her eyes concentrating on the boulder.

I thanked them, as Carly would've wanted me to, by placing another golden Zol Coin in each palm of the three elders and bowing graciously. Vera bowed and we were on our way through the mysterious phantom boulder.

We made our way out of the rural town and into the suburbs. From there we caught a ride into the city in the back of a pickup truck filled with fresh produce for sale at the farmers' market. There were no signs of war in this part of Zol Stria other than a few military vehicles and soldiers standing watch at the side of the street. We reached downtown in a short time and made our way to one of the high-rise apartment complexes where a friend of mine, Jultin, lived whenever he was in the city.

Jultin was a famous songwriter. After about three hundred years of composing and practicing music, he'd finally made it big about a hundred years ago. After he got noticed by a few of the Vičars, he'd secured patronage from the Great Houses and had built a large production business.

Jultin came from the lower Fae, and he had a difficult time swallowing down what he saw from the Council. He would always tell me how much he detested their abuse of power, which was why he was willing to help us.

The apartment was in the middle of the city. It was comfortable and modern with bamboo-themed decor. Ambient sounds spilled from hidden speakers in every room, subtle at times and then more obvious, to help visitors relax and disconnect. But more importantly, the apartment was a safe place to stay.

We were part of the resistance, after all, and if anyone identified us and turned us in to the Council, we would be crucified. He'd left me the keys in the mailbox and retreated to his home in the mountains, where I'd told him he should wait until this whole war was over. He was never much for fighting and was happy to heed my warning.

Tomorrow we would begin the search for Ixia. We'd discover exactly what she was up to and then, I would kill her.

❖

The next day, one of Jultin's showrunners arrived with a message. The runner told us that others in the resistance wanted to meet with us. Although the first thing I wanted to do was hunt down Ixia, I agreed to the meeting. We went to one of Jultin's five recording studios in the territory and met with a number of shop owners, professionals and other local dissenters. They filled us in on everything that had happened in Zol Stria after Sasha had taken off like a bat out of hell after the prophecy about her was revealed.

Zol Stria had been flung into a panic, shutting everything down and sending sentries to search for her from door to door. That was when the resistance activated. They had been waiting in the shadows, hoping the UnZol King would return. When word got out about the prophecy, they organized themselves. Many remained in Zol Stria, silent rebels of the Houses waiting for the right motivation to defect. The prophecy was just the sign from the stars they needed.

When Hun-Cane had found Sasha, he'd released a statement that all was under control and had showed images of her capture across the different territories. The Zol Council was convinced they had won.

As the Dark Zodiac armies fled to the Underworld to rally, the resistance remained and slowly began to organize. They said they watched as the Rot destroyed anything it touched, rendering crops unusable, polluting the air and water while making it toxic and inhabitable. What they didn't know was that Vucub-Cane was behind the Rot. It was only a distraction to keep Hun-Cane from searching for Sasha.

I explained to these rebel leaders what was behind the Rot. I told them how a few weeks ago, before the mating ritual, Vucub-Cane had come to Zol Stria under the guise of working with his brother to stop the Rot. When Hun-Cane finally had the time to check the holding cells, Sasha was gone. He went to tell his brother that Sasha was missing only to discover his brother had already left Zol Stria to return to the Underworld.

Rumors got out that Vucub-Cane's absence was because he was on the side of the resistance. When Hun-Cane tried to return to the Underworld, he was blocked out of his own realm with an ancient ward Vucub-Cane had been saving since they were children. That's when he put all the pieces together and realized what his brother had been up to.

"The rebel forces are organized. There are many of us who have infiltrated each of the Great Houses, all without them knowing it. When the Underworld attacks, we will be the ones to bring down those who oppress our families from the inside. We are in place and ready to fight," said a rebel that reminded me of an accountant from the mortal realm. Yet despite his buttoned-up appearance, I saw the real him. Under his crisp beige suit and behind his thin-framed glasses was a Fae with enough rage to fight hard for us.

"We'll need strong warriors on our side as the time nears," Vera said, commanding all eyes on her. Not only was she beautiful, but she led her army with a heart of steel.

"And when is that?" asked the accountant as mumbles stewed among them. No doubt they were all wondering the same thing.

"Surely before the next new moon," I said as I stuffed my hands in my pockets and leaned against the wall. I was far more casual than Vera would ever be in a situation like this. But then again, I had no interest in being a leader. There were others better suited for that than I was.

"Who is the leader of your group?" Vera asked. See? I knew she was a better leader than I was. Already asking the important questions.

"I am," the accountant said. "My name is Jayce."

"Ok then Jayce. We're going to need form a plan."

"Starting with where I can find Ixia," I added, straightening and approaching him.

"I got you," he said confidently.

I was all ears.

CHAPTER 16

There was no time for a long good-bye. No time for one final heated exchange between me and the UnZol King. No chance to feel his rippling muscles under my fingers, to watch as his dark, protective eyes lingered over my lips.

I could only kiss him feverishly. I could only wrap my arms around his center and squeeze. He wiped a tear away from my eye. A single, solitary tear that was filled with the sadness of finding him and having to leave him again so soon.

"I don't know why you're not sending someone else. Any one of your nagual unit would go in your place, you know that." His breath tickled my ear.

I rested my head on his chest. "It has to be me. I was the one pushing for this. I was the one who negotiated with the moon goddess. I have to be the one who takes responsibility for seeing this through."

I turned to face him now. My eyes scanning the sharp lines of his face, the dark beard he had begun to grow and the smooth texture of his lips. I was trying to hold every detail of him for as long as I could. When my eyes met his, all I saw was bitter fury festering underneath the surface. He wouldn't reveal himself to the others, but somehow, by the magic of our mating bond, I could still see it. I squeezed his hands so he knew I understood him. Then I whispered, "I'm sorry, but I am going."

"Then let me give you this." He removed a leather necklace from his pocket. There was a smooth, gray stone in the center of a brass frame.

"I thought these didn't exist. I thought they were a myth," I exclaimed, recognizing the stone from a minerals class back at the Academy.

"This is moonstone. Legend has it that an ancient quetzal brought this with it on a flight from the moon thousands of years ago. Let it be your guide on this journey."

I held the moonstone in my hand as I admired it. "I only heard about the quetzal briefly at the Academy and I don't remember much. What are they?" I asked.

"The quetzal are an extinct species of dragons that could fly in the furthest atmospheres of our planet. Some even said they flew through outer space. They were intelligent creatures and stored items in their pouches where they carried their young," he explained.

I lifted my hair so he could tie the leather string at the back of my neck. His broad arms around me were a comfort I hated to leave.

"It is time," I heard the goddess say from behind us. We were standing out on the terrace, and I wasn't sure what would happen next. When I'd tried to ask questions, I was given no answers. Balastar had said that others had been through this before, and I'd hoped to go to the great library to learn what had brought them there and gain any insight as to why they'd failed the trial. But there was no time for any of that. The moon goddess was impatient and she had made it clear I would go with her right now or never.

I faced the UnZol King again. His features were dark and fearsome, but he held a flame for me in those eyes.

"Nothing will happen to you that you can't come back from. I am proof of that. I will anchor you." His words trailed off as he disappeared before my eyes. Or I disappeared. I couldn't tell what was happening, only that I was no longer there in front of him. I was no longer anywhere. I was floating, moving as a soul, a spirit. I was certainly not a physical being, and now I was surrounded by a stark black darkness. Not the dark shadows and mist of my shadow weaving, but instead the clarity of a vacuum where nothing existed.

Then I felt myself shift into how I recognized myself. The darkness began to fade to light. I looked down and found my feet were planted on the ground, and when I raised my eyes, everything was pure, white light.

The moon goddess appeared before me. Her hair and gown floated around her as though there was no gravity to hold her to the ground. When she spoke, her voice was an echo and her eyes shone in a way not of any human or Fae I had ever seen.

"This is as far as I'll go with you on your journey. Either I meet you on the other side, or you never arrive. My one piece of advice is to find something to hold on to."

This was the first time I heard any sincerity in her voice and the first hint that she had any sense of humanity. Maybe it was because she knew I was doomed and was showing me some sort of kindness before my death. Or maybe it was because I had a fighting chance to come out of this trial with my life. I chose to believe the latter. This was not the end of my path. This was just the beginning.

I grasped at my neck for the moonstone. It warmed to my touch and when I released it, it was glowing.

If I was the UnZol King's anchor back into the world, he would be mine. I squeezed the moonstone tighter. This would be my path back home.

◆

I stood there in what was the brightest of the moon's light. She had said that I would have to transit the Moon Ward. From what I could tell, this felt like a full moon. Balastar thought that I would pass through some or all of the moon's phases as part of a trial. My eyes stung from the glow and I had to hold my hand over my eyes to protect them from the glare of the constant bright light. I searched my mind for everything I knew about the moon's phases and what part they could play in a trial such as this one.

It was then that my thoughts began to overtake me. They came flooding in uncontrollably fast. One after another. Every kind gesture I'd ever made to another person. Every time I'd appreciated and showed gratitude for another. There were those moments where I found the world so incredibly beautiful that all I did was soak in its wonder: the majestic colors of a sunset, the glistening peaks of waves in the ocean, the dance of tiny faeries tumbling together on a field of poppy flowers. There was so much beauty in the world that sometimes I felt my heart would burst from enjoying it all.

And then there was that love for others that squeezed my heart and warmed my chest. My mate, the UnZol King, who in such a short time had filled me with a love like I had never known. My nagual family, who had been through everything with me, and whom I would do anything for. Damian, who had proven to me time and again that people could change and new relationships could be formed. And like my family back home, those that I'd left behind to become part of the Fae, they were there for me when I'd been at my absolute worse.

In the blinding light of the moon, I could feel this powerful love thrum through every single part of me, threatening to make me burst at the thought that I was lucky enough to have so much love in my life.

I quite enjoyed this. This was so lovely. Such a bright and happy place; anyone would want to come here and bask in this beauty.

And there, sitting on a small white boulder several feet from me, appeared a woman. She was so beautiful. Her face was positively glowing. Her smile was perfection. Every light-brown hair was perfectly in place. I walked toward her. She gave me a warm, welcoming smile. I didn't know why but I sat on the floor next to her and listened as she began to sing. She sang chords I couldn't even imagine. Her beautiful voice filled me with even more love.

Then she began to speak. She told me I was amazing. Capable of all manner of wonderful things. She told me I could have everything. Do anything. I began sobbing with emotion. I told her about the people I'd hurt. The monsters I'd killed and the mistakes I'd made along the way to becoming who I was now. She welcomed me with loving arms, wrapping me in warmth and safety.

In that moment, there was no safer place to be in the entire universe, so my aura naturally released. It was something I hadn't done in a very long time. I didn't bother putting up a deflector spell, for what harm could come to me now?

And just as her cloak covered me, bright white fangs snapped out of her porcelain face. They looked so wrong surrounded by soft, pink lips. I barely realized what was happening, my guard completely down, my aura flashing, and no deflector spell in place to shield me.

But she's not a monster, she's an angel! I was so confused.

I scuttled backwards like a startled crab, barely escaping her bite. The flood of emotion that had dampened my cheeks also made me too weak to stand. I almost fell limp to the floor, my heart squeezing in my chest for trusting this Fae who I'd thought would never hurt me. Her words had been so loving, her embrace so kind. How could she be anything other than the pure, abundant love I wanted her to be?

She leaped toward me. My instincts took over and I rolled my body to the left, barely avoiding her.

Then it came to me. *I'm still in a trial, and this is only my first test.*

The fogginess of my mind began to clear. I quickly checked my emotions and rose to a standing position within seconds. I called the shadows toward me, retracted my aura, and raised a shadow shield within seconds to protect me from the wrath of whatever this thing was.

The beautiful fanged woman hissed.

"I've seen your kind before," I spat. "You use the light to get people to be vulnerable, to open up, to create a false sense of safety just so you can take what you want from them. I've known people like you my whole life. Only instead of fangs they used their words to tear people down. Or they try to manipulate and control you, which is even worse because before you know it, they've already taken everything. At least I can see your fangs before they pierce my skin. You won't be taking anything at all from me. Not today. Not ever."

The Fae spread her arms wide and lunged at me, but I was faster. I pulled in the dark to shift into my jaguar form, but I couldn't do it. Something was blocking my shift. I managed to raise claws to my hands and jaguar fangs to my teeth.

I took a swipe at her as I hissed, slicing into her chest and arms. Though I felt my claws cut into a physical form, no blood spilled from her body. She simply disappeared, fading into the white space from where she came.

I was alone again. My heart thumped hard in my chest and my mind raced. If this was any indication of the trials I had remaining, I'd have to be ready for anything. My skills in physical combat and magic wouldn't be enough.

In fact, my mind had to be the strongest of all my skills if I was going to make it out of here alive.

CHAPTER 17

DAMIAN

The energy of Zol Stria had shifted. There were armed Fae patrolling the streets and winged Fae on surveillance in the skies. Zol Stria had also adopted much of the technology of the mortal realm; hidden video cameras were everywhere. I raised a transfiguration spell to alter my appearance so I could go undetected in the city.

"The transfiguration spell didn't work on you," I told Vera after several failed attempts.

"I told you it wouldn't work. Your spells don't work on elves. It's ok, I don't think anyone will recognize me anyway. My people are of the forest. Not many of us live in the city. I don't think I'll run into anyone I know." She shrugged.

"Fine. I guess it will have to be this way for now, anyway. Unless I can find a way around it."

We ventured out into the crisp, cool day. It was late fall and the chill of winter was beginning to creep in. I zipped up my coat as we headed out of the apartment building and onto the street. I had chosen the appearance of an older man, seven hundred Fae years around the sun, forty in human years. Vera told me I looked like the sexy older professor all the college girls would pine over. I was pleased because it was exactly what I was going for.

We had to move fast as we didn't have many options when it came to trapping Ixia. We headed straight to the Aquarius Academy greenhouse where the rebels had told us she was producing biomagical weapons. I promised them some intel on whatever it was she was doing in there, just as long as I got to take my revenge on her right after. If the rumors of the weapons she was developing were true, we wouldn't stand a chance against their attacks.

We arrived on campus and, although there were guards everywhere, no one gave us a second look. If my identity had been detected, we would have been stopped by now. I breathed a sigh of relief and headed farther into the campus. Before we reached the greenhouse, Vera turned to me to say good-bye, concern in her eyes. "I'm going to find my family. You'll be fine, right?"

"Yes, I'll be fine. But why don't you just wait for me to finish this and let me come with you when I'm done?"

"Just because something happened to Lily doesn't mean it will happen to me. I need to find my family now and you need to do this." Her eyes darted in the direction of the greenhouse then returned to me.

I pressed my lips to hers and held her close. She placed her hand on my chest and fell into my embrace.

"Be safe," I whispered.

"I will," she said.

With that, she turned and walked away.

I made my way to the greenhouse, passing students on the way to class. Life was going on as usual on this campus. It was as though House Aquarius didn't see the Dark Zodiac as a threat.

As I approached the building, I took in the glass walls that went up about three stories to form the rounded ceiling. I opened the double glass doors to reveal meticulous rows of various plants. They were organized by species and several rows of them were exactly the same. A handful of dryads tended to the plants with care.

One of the dryads wore gloves that went all the way to her elbows, a protective plastic apron and a clear face mask. She had removed a large brown fruit that grew abundantly on a row of leafy green bushes. I hadn't seen a fruit like that before so I watched as she placed it carefully on the counter and cut it open. A bright-orange liquid spilled out of it. I could smell the potency of the contents from where I was standing all the way across the greenhouse and wondered what the hell they were growing in here.

"Professor Gussman, how are you? I thought you were at Capricorn Academy these days. So nice to see you back here," one of the dryads said. She held a pink-flowered plant in her hand.

Shit! I didn't realize I'd taken on the appearance of Professor Gussman.

He'd been my Magical Sciences professor when I'd done an exchange study at Virgo Academy all those years ago. All the girls had crushed endlessly over him and I remembered thinking how when I got older, I would be a handsome professor just like him.

"Oh yes," I said, then remembered he had a slight British accent after years of working at Oxford University on the other side of the Gates. Professors often took roles in the mortal realm so they could stay connected to the latest academic trends among humans. "Great to see you, dear. So, you've secured an apprenticeship here. Well done. Remind me of your name?"

She batted her eyes at me and smiled. "I'm Maribel. And thank you. Actually, they've recruited all the senior- and junior-level dryads to accelerate the growth of these plants in the greenhouse," she said proudly, gesturing to the expanse of plants behind her.

"I would like to congratulate Ixia for her highly innovative approach in cultivating all of this. Is she around?" I scanned the greenhouse hopefully, plastering a pleasant grin on my face to make sure I seemed harmless.

"Well today is your lucky day." She scanned me up and down for several heartbeats longer than I would have expected. Her eyes lingered around my chest and lower abdominal area as though she was imagining what lay underneath. "She's just over there in the laboratory, inspecting her latest creation. The *Siniluios mortis*. That's the scientific name of the plant she genetically modified." The trim, blonde dryad leaned in, looping her hand through my arm. "Come, let me take you to her."

"Sure then, ok. You lead the way." I chuckled slightly at her gesture. Meanwhile I fought against the compounded rage toward Ixia that festered and boiled just underneath the surface.

As we approached the far end of the greenhouse, the dryad stopped halfway to Ixia and asked if she could call me some time.

"Maybe you could be my mentor?" she said, wetting her lips and gazing up at me.

I glanced impatiently over at Ixia, wondering if this tedious conversation would keep me from getting to her before she left. To my relief, Ixia was fully immersed in whatever it was she was doing and didn't seem to be going anywhere anytime soon.

I fumbled out words and pretended to be flattered. I imagined a version of me at another time would have allowed someone as beautiful as this dryad to distract me. Another me would take her number and keep this transfiguration spell going long enough to roleplay a one-night stand with this gorgeous Fae. For the first time in a very long time, I wondered how Vera would feel if I slept with someone else. I wondered if it would hurt her. That thought alone was enough to make me pass up a steamy hookup with this female.

"Sorry, but I've stopped mentoring students for a while. Also, I believe you would be better suited with a professor at this academy."

She looked downright crushed, but I was pleased to find no lingering regret simmering within me. Now that she was delt with, it was time for me to get to work.

It was hard to find Ixia beautiful like I used to. I'd once found her radiant, golden-brown skin, her soft, light-brown curls and amber eyes irresistible. Now she downright disgusted me. It was even harder to keep my hands from reaching around her throat as I got within a few feet of her.

"Headmistress, you have a guest," the dryad said.

"Don't you know better?" Ixia snapped. "Get him out of here and have him put on the protective gear. You too. You should never enter my laboratory dressed like that. You'll both contaminate my samples and probably get yourself killed in the process."

The dryad cast her eyes down and scurried us out of the lab. She retrieved protective gear that she had me put on and didn't return with me inside the lab.

Ixia barely acknowledged me when I returned to her work area. She was looking through a microscope amidst a rather elaborate arrangement of scientific apparatuses. "Professor Gussman, my apologies for her lack of professionalism. They've sent me all these inexperienced students and, quite frankly, I'm sick of babysitting them." She met my eyes and they seemed to glimmer at the sight of me. "And to what do I owe the pleasure of this visit?"

Before I could answer, she returned her gaze to the microscope and her analysis. Then she reached for a glass vial and took a small sample of the bright-orange liquid that spilled out from the center of the brown fruit and placed it inside the tube.

"I was just visiting Aquarius and wanted to stop by and say hello," I said casually. One side of her mouth curled upward into a smirk and she narrowed her eyes as she looked at me. I was grateful she couldn't read minds; if she could, she'd figure out who I was very quickly.

"Oh really? Just stop by and say hello like we're old friends? You think the other Houses haven't sent their own solicitors to stop by and say hello? At least they come bearing gifts," she scoffed and focused again on closing the glass vial and bringing it to a wooden test tube rack. I assumed this was where she tested the chemical components of her plants.

"Capricorn Academy has a lot to offer. Rather than bring you a gift today, I wanted to learn more about what you needed and how we can build a stronger partnership, should you also be willing to share your research with us." I absolutely hated that I had to dance around things with her. But bringing her to the slow and painful death she deserved right here and now, like I wanted to, would be a quick way to get myself killed. She was a powerful mage who had the advantage here in her domain, and when I assassinated her, I had to be absolutely sure that I would win.

"Well, that sounds impressive, but I'm in the middle of this analysis. I can't discuss this now." She gave me a sly side eye and the hint of a smile. Because I knew her all too well, I knew this was her way of flirting.

"And now I'm curious, what kind of analysis is that?"

Her eyes darted around the laboratory and she whispered conspiratorially, "Oh, I can't tell you that. It's top secret."

"I promise, I won't tell a Zol." I placed my hand on my chest and gave her an innocent look.

"Well, if I tell you, you must swear to secrecy with binding magic."

"Fine, binding magic it is. And I'll sweeten the deal if you let me buy you a drink whenever you're done here." If Professor Gussman could seduce that hot little dryad, he might have a chance with this plant-demon.

"It's a deal." She removed her glove and held her hand out to me. I cringed internally at the thought of touching her. This had to be the most utterly painful attempt at acting I had ever done.

My mouth soured as we clasped our hands together and dark shadows curled around our arms, locking in the curse that would prevent me from speaking of this. If I even attempted to speak of what I saw here, my mind would erase the memory of it before the words could leave my mouth.

"Well, if you must know, curious professor—and you should want to know because this will be all the rage the moment I release the formula to our forces." She replaced her glove and picked up the glass tube with the bright-orange liquid she'd sampled from the inside the fruit. She held it up in the light and turned it this way and that. The bright-orange substance seemed to glow maliciously as she did. "This is Zoltoxin. The main ingredient is derived from a genetically modified *Siniluios mortis* plant grown here, in this very greenhouse. And the formula is based on a combination of ancient botany, alchemy and new technology in biogenetics. The solution to all our problems is right here." Ixia set the tube down carefully inside a glass encasement then locked it with a key in a necklace she wore.

"This substance is incredibly potent," she continued, "and it has the ability to temporarily neutralize the magical abilities of your opponent. You only have to place a single drop of the substance on their skin."

I kept my eyes from growing wide and instead forced a proud smile on my face. The Fae had been trying for years to come up with a way to neutralize magical powers outside of the Underworld's prison system. Ixia had created biomagical Zol warfare.

"Well done, Headmistress. That is quite impressive." I inspected her laboratory more closely, squinting as I looked at the various vials and gaping as though impressed at her genius innovations. But really, I just wanted to grab the poison and pour it all over her.

She gloated arrogantly over her creation as she walked out of the laboratory without so much as a word. Through the glass, I watched as she removed her gloves, washed her hands, and took off all her protective gear.

Well, ok, then. I guess we're done in here.

A few moments later I left the laboratory and did the same. She had begun to leave the greenhouse ahead of me. I picked up my pace and caught up to her. She stopped abruptly and turned to me.

"I'll meet you for happy hour at Delicias de Aquarius. They have the best sangria in all Zol Stria," she said. "See you then."

This lady was all business.

"Yes, great. See you then." I smirked and she hurried off somewhere.

In just a few hours, she would be wishing she'd never fucked with me or my family.

CHAPTER 18

White faded to pitch black and the cold began to set in. The same frigid, bone-chilling cold I'd felt when I first met the moon goddess.

This must be the phase of the new moon, the utter dark. I expected my chances were better at facing the dark since this was my very nature. I brought fire to my palms and lit them bright so the warmth from the flames would keep me from freezing. I was ever so grateful for my fire element at a time like this.

I caught sight of the moonstone around my neck and noticed it was glowing. I wondered why for a moment, but I didn't allow it to continue distracting me. The more pressing task at hand was searching the new moon's darkness for my next challenge. Would the dark try to manipulate me like the light had? Or would a dark monster come and take a swipe at me from among the endless shadows that existed here?

Howls and screeches could be heard off in the distance. A fog began to roll in from the east. I stepped back. With nothing to protect me on either side, I had to search all around me and be ready for anything.

That was when I began to hear little feet scurrying about. Something small was running in that fog. Not at me, but to the left, then to the right, then behind me. I spun around, shifting my eyes to my jaguar's and honing my night vision, trying catch sight of what was running around me. But they were too fast, or I was too slow. I just couldn't see it.

"Hey. Hey, who's there?" I asked, my voice firm and full of authority.

More running could be heard. *What are they?*

Then I heard someone crying. A child screamed. I wanted to run toward the sound, but I hesitated. This place was full of trickery. I wasn't falling for it again.

"Help," a young girl's voice called out. "Please help me."

I approached the sound slowly and an old Buick sedan appeared out of the gloom. When I looked inside the window, what I saw made my mouth gape open and my fire disappear.

This can't be. I can't be seeing this.

I turned away and rubbed my still-hot hand on my forehead as vomit tried to come up my throat.

"Please. Help my mommy," the voice said again.

Tears threatened to well up in my eyes. I peeked over my shoulder and looked at the car again, my eyebrows furrowed in confusion, my mouth open wide in disbelief.

That was nine-year-old me sitting there in the passenger side of the car with my mother's head on my lap. I was brushing her bleach-blonde hair away from her face where she had a huge black eye from where my father had punched her earlier that evening. I was so little, so afraid back then. My mother's phone rang and nine-year-old me answered it.

"Hola, Tia Lily." Her voice was soft and nearly sobbing. "Sí. Mami is here."

My mother stirred and sat up, grabbing the phone from the young hand. "Sí. Everything is fine," she mumbled. "No. We aren't coming to live with you. We'll be fine right here."

My mother's eyes darted to the girl then to the back seat where the young version of my older brother was curled up and sleeping. "Listen, all that talk about shamans and jaguars needs to stop. You sound crazy. I'd rather sleep on the side of the street than send my child to live with a crazy person." She hung up and my aunt called right back. My mother wouldn't answer.

My mother had never shared my aunt's beliefs about the world of Zol Stria and, later, my role in it. Her refusal to believe had gotten worse after she'd met my father and he'd isolated her from the family. I wasn't sure if it was to please him, or because she truly just didn't believe in any of this, but she'd always been against it.

This was all her fault.

It'd been my mother this whole time keeping me from my fate. Choosing to live with a man who abused her and forced us out on the street, denying me the one person in the world who could help me become the Fae warrior I needed to be.

Claws sprang out of my hands.

I ran around to the driver's side and tried to yank open the car door, but it wouldn't open. The young version of my mother didn't even see me; she just went on as though I wasn't banging on her door or her window. I screamed. I just wanted to get to that phone and speak to Lily. I wanted to tell her everything that had happened to me and that I wished she'd never gotten on that plane.

I sobbed into my hands and screamed. Kicked at my mother's car door and slashed at it with my jaguar claws. But the door wouldn't budge under my blows; I didn't even make a scratch in it. I snarled at the woman in the car: the beast I couldn't fight because she was more in my mind than anything that existed in real life.

I was in a whirlwind of all the emotions I had felt back then mixed with the fear and frustrations I had now. How much of what had happened when I was a girl was I still hanging on to? How much of that was the reason I was here now, watching the young me having to grow up too fast?

As I stood there, I caught sight of the moonstone around my neck in the reflection of the car window. It was glowing again. I closed my hand around it and felt it warm my skin. That was when I realized how cold I was. I had stopped harnessing fire. I'd been distracted by this thing that happened to me so long ago that I'd forgotten the freezing temperatures. I looked at my hands; they were turning purple from the cold. My teeth chattered.

I raised the fire within me again and used it to warm me. I could have died just now. I needed to let go of the past. With that single thought, the car drove away and I was left in the pitch black of the new moon, no longer cold.

For what felt like hours I stood there looking out into the deafening darkness of the new moon. I knew enough from my zodiac studies that the new moon meant new beginnings. You could harness the energy of this moon phase by focusing on the things you wanted to happen to you, or for you, in the weeks to come. And when you truly let go of the things holding you back, they would no longer hold any more power over you. I promised myself right then I would let it all go. I would forgive my mother for the choices I thought were wrong so they wouldn't be a burden to me.

A sliver of silver appeared at the far end of the darkness. It was the crescent moon. I ran toward it as fast as I could. It must be the next moon phase I had to pass through.

I wondered if I would have to go through all of them. I didn't know how much more of these emotions I would have to face, or how the moon would toy with me next. All I knew was that I had to get to the end of these trials alive.

There was way too much at stake.

CHAPTER 19

DAMIAN

I f the vials weren't heavily guarded with wards in the laboratory, I would have grabbed one while I was in there. As I was leaving the greenhouse, I ran into the dryad Maribel, who was crying on the veranda when I walked by. The veranda was tucked away at the very back of the greenhouse, facing the Whispering Woods.

I sat next to her on the bench. She gave me a welcoming smile and scooted closer to me. I draped an arm around her. "It's alright. I'm sure whatever it is you're dealing with, it'll be all right."

She sobbed into my jacket then lifted her face and kissed me with wet tears streaking down her cheeks. Forgetting myself, I caressed her for a moment, then gently pulled away as any man of my stature would.

"I'm sorry," I said. "I didn't mean to lead you on. It is highly inappropriate for staff to fraternize with students. I could lose my job and you could get kicked out."

No longer tear-ridden, she raised a deflector spell with a dark tint that covered us completely. With her hands still wrapped around my waist, she looked at me intently while biting her lower lip.

"How did you raise this shield?" I asked, trying to keep this casual. It was impressive to see her use this skill at such a young age. This kind of shield was from a spell that could take at least a century to perfect.

"I read all about it in one of your published journals and practiced every day until I got it right. I have to tell you, Professor, I've been a fan of you and your work since I was a little girl." She giggled and I shifted, uncomfortable at how close we were. Vera's face flashed in my mind. I wanted to see where things would go with her, not this young college girl who thought I was someone else.

"This will be our little secret," she said and kissed me again. This time searching my mouth with her tongue, she pressed her full chest against mine and gripped my shoulders.

"I'm sorry." I pulled away again and released a breath. I tried to stand but she held on to me tightly.

"I have something for you." She reached into her jacket pocket, pulled out a glass vial of the orange Zoltoxin, and handed it to me. "I believe you came here looking for this, so I brought some for you."

As I inspected the liquid, she pulled me toward her again, eagerly gripping me, kissing my neck and grabbing my now-very-hard dick. It was instinct for me, to get this hard with such a beautiful woman in front of me. Vera and I aren't in a relationship yet, after all. I don't even know if she feels the same way that I do. And there's the fact that I just got my hands on the very thing I was sent here to retrieve. I can't blow my cover now.

"Binding magic," I breathed. Maybe just this one last time would be ok, especially if no one could find out. "You are not to tell a soul that you gave this to me, or that we fraternized."

"Anything." Maribel smiled widely. "You have no idea how long I've fantasized about this very moment."

The moment our magic bonded, she pulled her shirt off, revealing her white lace bra that she quickly unstrapped and flung to the side. Maribel's breasts were full, her nipples round and firm, her skin tan and smooth. She grabbed at my pullover sweater, yanking it over my head then unbuttoning my shirt and running her hands all over my chest. Maribel placed her breast inches from my mouth and I took her in, gracing her nipple with my tongue, kissing the firm, rounded flesh.

Straddling me, she reached her hands down to my pants and unbuckled them. Taking me in her hands, she continued to stroke as she slipped off my lap and between my legs to take me in her mouth. I moaned with pleasure; she groaned in response. Her wet lips tugged with pressure, her hand pulling and working me up and down.

I was her fantasy and this was all lust.

She stood, pulling her panties off from underneath her skirt, and climbed on top of me. Her curves were smooth, her youth evident. I slid into her and placed my hands on her hips as she groaned with pleasure. She rocked up and down, her skin electric with desire and my mouth wrapped around one breast as they swayed. Over and over she found that place that made her quiver and moan with excitement, her eyes wild and free until she reached the peak and gushed over me.

I kissed her and groaned, flipping her over to brace her knees on the bench as she put her hands against the wall. I swept her skirt up and paused; the curve of her waist to her ass was lovely. Then I entered her from the back and was on the brink of thrusting as she backed her ass into me. But I couldn't imagine this professor being that aggressive, so instead I pulsed until I reached my peak.

I stopped by the apartment before meeting Ixia so I could wash Maribel's smell off me. That mage's ability to pick up scent was otherworldly. I quickly changed into a fresh set of professor-like clothing and stored the vial of Zoltoxin in the apartment. I still didn't know how to use it and, given the complex chemical compounds of the substance, I didn't want to take any chances until I understood it better. Any mistakes could be catastrophic, for me and anyone I was near when I used it.

Relief washed over me when I realized Vera was still out getting her family. I wouldn't want her to pick up on Maribel's scent either. I immediately stuffed the clothing in the washing machine and ran the load. It was completely unlike me to even care what a female thought about what I did with my own free time. But for some reason, Vera was different.

I wasn't too worried about Maribel. When she'd left, she'd given me a sly smile like she'd just gotten exactly what she wanted and as I held the Zoltoxin in my hand, I'd realized that we both had. It surprised me that she didn't ask me to meet with her again. I wasn't too worried if she began to stalk the real Professor Gussman about getting together, either, because after all this was done and the Zol Council was taken down, I wouldn't care at all what anyone thought.

Anyone except Vera, I guess. I shook it off. I didn't even know why I was thinking about her so much. I was sure she wasn't thinking about me in the same way. She must have a hundred elven males better suited to her than me. Well, even if she did, I would still take my shot with her. And even if she shot me down, it would be worth it.

As I approached the restaurant, I admired the colonial Spanish buildings that lined the city streets. The city reminded me a lot of Barcelona with the orange barreled roofs and the cobblestone streets. The restaurant was nestled at the end of a curved street. Tables were placed out under umbrellas and the smell of grilled meat and Spanish spices filled my lungs.

There, at a table in the far corner of the terrace, was Ixia. She was early, already sitting with a pitcher of sangria and two glasses on the table.

"I took the liberty of ordering my favorite drink here," she said, and I instantly didn't trust it. This drink could be laced with poison; the last drink she'd given me had that put me under an enamor spell.

"Oh this looks fantastic. Thank you." I sat in the chair across from her and poured myself a glass of the deep-red beverage. I waved my hand quickly over the glass to cast a neutralizing spell over it and hoped she didn't notice.

We sat and exchanged small talk before she asked me, "So, Professor, do tell me, what does Capricorn Academy have to offer Aquarius? What is it you can give us that I can't get from anywhere else?" Her eyes were bright and wide as she placed her chin in her hand and flashed me her pearly white teeth.

"I... We..." I fumbled my words. I couldn't feel my tongue.

"Oh. I'm afraid I can't understand you. What was that now?"

I reached for a cup of water and hesitated. She had done something to me with that sangria! I tried to get up. I could go to the bar and ask for water there. But as soon as I placed my hands on the table to stand, I felt my knees buckle underneath me. I was paralyzed.

"Now I know you're not Professor Gussman. Shame on you for assuming I couldn't see that you had a transfiguration spell in place. I'll have you know that very little gets past me. So I'm going to take you back to my private villa and when the Zoltoxin wears off, you can release the spell and show me who you really are." Ixia sat back in her chair and my mind raced to find a way out of this, but I couldn't move. "Besides that, I called Capricorn Academy after I saw you. Professor Gussman is still there, giving class today."

"It's me." My tongue felt swollen in my mouth and my voice sounded muffled. I tried to tell her who I really was but it was an epic fail because of the poison.

"You're impossible to understand." She rolled her eyes impatiently and drank from her glass. "I may have used too much Zoltoxin; you really shouldn't be paralyzed like this. I may have to adjust the formula." Ixia leaned in and studied me closer. She plucked a phone out of her purse and made a phone call. "Guido, I need you to help me take care of a friend of mine."

I tried everything I could to move my arms, to cast a protective spell and even speak a few words clearly. Nothing worked.

"You are officially one of the first few Fae to experience the effects of a full dosage of Zoltoxin. Did I forget to mention that the potion is undetectable by traditional scans? That spell neutralizers don't work on it?" As she laughed at her own joke, I was reminded of everything I hated about this woman. She had to kill me right now. That was the only way she could possibly get out of me slicing her into tiny pieces while she was still alive and feeding her skin to the crows.

Guido showed up moments later. The heavy-set, Armani-wearing thug lifted me from my chair and wrapped an arm around my waist so that he could practically carry me out of the restaurant and into the Bentley he had idling close by. Ixia slid into the back seat next to me. During the whole ride to her villa, she rambled on and on about everything she thought of the prophecy, the UnZol King and "the ridiculous war" that the Dark Zodiac was sure to lose over Zol Stria.

I seethed as I sat there, unable to do or say anything. Somehow, I would get out of this. I had to.

CHAPTER 20

The closer I got to the silver light, the louder the sounds from within it became.

The scene before me was complete chaos. People were running everywhere. There were familiar faces: the Dark Zodiac shamans and mages I'd met during my time in the Underworld, the professors at Aries Academy and their students. As they ran, they seemed not to see me.

I saw civilians, those people of the town who hadn't taken any sides, and suddenly my world got larger. It was as though I was placed right back on the boardwalk of the town where I'd lived in Aries for the past few years. Yet the sky had darkened and a light-crimson shade blanketed the land.

I looked up into the sky and saw the moon undergoing a lunar eclipse.

As my eyes were focused on the sky, I saw a dragon with the wingspan of a football field fly overhead. He released a roar that shot thunder and electricity into the air.

Suddenly, Zol Stria forces began marching through the streets and a voice resounded from a loud speaker, "All citizens of Zol Stria must convene at the town square immediately."

Fae started filing out into the street from their townhouses, villas and apartments. They quickly exited the shops, left their cars parked wherever they could and approached the center in swarms. I snatched a hoodie from a local shop before it closed and put it on, making sure the hoodie covered my head and face as much as possible. I was the Queen of the Dark Zodiac, a very public traitor of Zol Stria. The last thing I wanted was to be recognized.

The faint crimson light had been cast over everything and anxious energy rippled through the air. The town square had a small amphitheater where local actors, musicians and others would perform on the weekends and special holidays. But tonight there would be no special music.

I could see five figures up on the stage kneeling with their hands tied behind their backs. It was difficult to see what was happening through the crowd. My heart began to pound in my chest as I worked my way through the bodies that were filling up the square.

My eyes opened wide when I saw who they were. Jenna, Lex, Bjorn, Axel, Andres and Eliana were there, captured. Their faces were cold and hard as their eyes stared straight ahead. At once they were both steel and fury.

For a moment I forgot this was a trial. I released a ragged breath and reached my hand around the moonstone, its warmth reminding me that this wasn't real. It was only another attempt at getting me to fall into some kind of trap.

Five Zol Council soldiers, each dressed in black battle gear with a white zodiac wheel on their arm, walked up behind the members of my nagual unit. I braced myself, because this did not look good.

"This is what happens to traitors," said the headmaster of Aries Academy. The crowd jeered and booed in agreement. "And this is how we weed out our enemies."

The soldiers raised their swords and, on the headmaster's command, they each swiped one fatal blow to the nagual necks, decapitating them instantly. As their blood spilled and their bodies thumped on the wooden stage, I squeezed my eyes shut, wishing this horrific scene to hurry up and be over.

I stifled a scream and ground my teeth. *This is just a trial! A horrible nightmare. It isn't real.*

My knuckles turned white from squeezing the moonstone so tight.

Damian was shoved onto the stage next. His hair was a mess for the first time ever, his beard uncombed and his clothes wrinkled and dirty as though he'd been held captive for some time. He lifted his eyes to the crowd and scanned the faces, landing directly on me.

Sasha, this isn't a dream. This is real. Run.

His words came down through the bond just like before I was mated to the UnZol King. I could hear him clearly. It was his voice, I knew it. I called the shadows to me instinctively. My rage had built up so much, I just had to launch myself at them. Rip those soldiers limb from limb. My clothes shredded as I shifted into my black jaguar. Creature of darkness and shadows, nightmares and mist.

I ran to the stage and attacked a soldier, ripping his chest open in one slash and moving on to the next one. I was so massive in my jaguar size I could take down eight full-grown Fae males at one time. And I did. I took them all out. Piercing skin, cracking bones and ripping off limbs. When I was finished, the crowd began to close in. Many of them took turns taking shots with their elemental magic at me and yet it made no difference in my jaguar skin.

Damian got up and ran with me off the stage and into the city.

She trapped me, Sasha. Ixia trapped me. She has a poison that can kill us all.

I heard his words through our bond but kept running. *We've got to get out of here.*

I ran as fast as I could for the forest outside of town, listening for his footsteps behind me until I heard him stop. I turned around and saw that he had been attacked by a huge Zolari Demon with steel for teeth and claws.

Damian, I screamed as the creature ripped into him. Intestines spilled out of his belly. Screams of agony left his throat as I lunged after the demon, locking my sharp fangs around its neck and flinging it to the ground with a heavy thump. The taste of Zolari Demon blood was fresh on my tongue and I wanted more. I clawed and carved into the fleshy black insides of this gruesome creature.

When I was finished with him, I ran off into the forest to escape the crowd that was closing in behind me. My face and neck stung with every step, warm blood dripping into my eyes. That was when I realized the creature had wounded me.

My feet pounded the hard rocks of the ground. I wanted to feel every sting, every pointy stone, every stick and thorn. I ran until my legs were prodded, sore and the city was far, far behind me. I couldn't cry in my jaguar skin, so when I got to the safe house we had in the forest, I shifted and went inside. I cast a protective deflector spell all around the house and its clearing and changed into the jeans, T-shirt and Converses I had stored there. My mind filled with an incessant roaring. I pressed my palms over my ears but it did nothing to stop the thoughts from pounding in over and over. I cried my eyes out on the couch until I couldn't cry anymore.

I didn't know how long I sat curled up on the couch with my head in my hands, but after the sun had long set and the sky was black as night, I opened my palms. They were sticky from my own blood that had not stopped pouring from a cut over my eye. I went to the bathroom and inspected the wound. It was deep and wide and it stretched over my left eye and down my cheek. The one on my neck was severely deep, too. Wincing in pain, I stitched myself together.

Fuck. What is happening?

My throat felt tight and I could barely breathe. I struggled for air as my chest heaved and my mind went into a panic. I didn't save them. They were stupid.

They were so fucking stupid.

My nagual unit had trusted me and they shouldn't have. I'd gotten Zayne killed and now the rest of them were gone. I was the one who'd run from the prophecy, not them. I was the one who'd mated with the UnZol King. They didn't deserve that brutal death. They should never had tried to save me from the prison. I paced the room and tried to remember something Balastar had told me about hanging on to things. What was it I was supposed to do?

I lost something. I feel like I lost something.

I reached my hand around my neck. I scanned my body. Balastar had given me something, at least I thought he had. Thoughts of sadness kept racing in, faster than I could think of anything else.

In an instant, I couldn't remember anything before this moment. All my thoughts were jumbled up in a stew of sadness. Boiling and brimming, spilling over for all the love I had lost today. It was a festering sadness that had started when Zayne died. I had buried it deep, but it was always there, simmering beneath the surface. Today that sadness multiplied and filled my soul entirely.

Not a fragment of my existence wasn't overwhelmed with grief and suffering as I fell to the floor, curled my knees up to my chest and rocked my body back and forth.

There was only room for anguish in this new place in my mind. I would forget and be forgotten, because it was all I had ever deserved anyway.

CHAPTER 21

DAMIAN

I had to give it to Ixia, she was always prepared. Guido dragged me to her private villa where she had her own garden, laboratory and living area. She had him place me in a special chamber two levels below the main floor. It was fitted with glass walls all around and furnished with a large, comfortable chair and a small table with a few books stacked on it. There was also a large plastic cup filled with water. As soon as she closed the door and locked it, I realized this was a cell.

"I believe in treating my prisoners with dignity. Unless they lose when we play the truth-or-lies game." Ixia stood at the other side of the glass from me, casually assessing me as if I was a lab rat.

I sat motionless in the chair.

"I'm going to leave you here for a while. Once you can start moving your limbs, you'll be able to drink from that cup to cleanse you. Then you'll release the transfiguration spell and show me who you really are or stay in there until you die. Whichever comes first. Guido will keep you company while I'm gone." She strutted out of the observation room.

The observation room wasn't sparse like the kind you saw on TV. There was a large bamboo bookshelf on one wall and comfortable armchairs facing the glass wall. An end table separated the chairs and the floor was covered in a blue-and-white patterned rug. Several indoor plants were tastefully placed around the space. It seemed cozy, which was a huge contradiction for a place that held people captive and interrogated them.

Guido plopped himself down in one of the armchairs directly across from me, his huge frame taking up the entire breadth of the chair. It seemed I would be here for a while, so I closed my eyes and took a nap.

When I awoke, I was able to move my fingers and arms. Guido was napping himself, his head bent over his chest, his snores releasing in a steady rhythm.

I was tempted to drink from the cup Ixia had left for me. I wanted to hurry up and get this poison out of my system. But now I didn't even trust that the water was safe. I ran a series of neutralizing spells on it before I picked it up. I sniffed it. I set it down and paced the room, rubbing my beard and debating on what to do.

"Just drink it," I heard a raspy voice say. I turned and found Guido with his eyes wide open. He reminded me of a bulldog. "Save us all some time and drink it."

I considered him, then glanced back to the drink. If I didn't drink it, this would all take longer, whether or not it worked to flush my system.

"Bottoms up, then." I raised the glass toward him and brought it to my lips. I drank it down in a few quick gulps, but my thirst wasn't satisfied. I set the cup back down on the table and it refilled automatically. I drank it down again. After a few glasses, I used the toilet. This went on for several hours until I could feel my magic starting to return.

The first thing I did was test the wards in this room. It was some sort of isolation chamber where the magic I used would be isolated to this room only. I couldn't extend my magic outside of these walls. So that left me with only one choice: tell her the truth of who I was and hope that my irresistible charm still worked on.

"Oh, Damian!" Ixia raised her hands to her mouth as soon as she saw me. "Oh my god. I can't believe it's you." She threw her jacket and purse down on the chair beside Guido and approached the glass wall. Her eyes were so much warmer than I thought they would be.

"I don't know whether to kill you or kiss you. After all that's happened, and the battle in Miami..." She scanned my face as though it held all the answers. Ixia inhaled deeply. "You hurt me, deeply. I thought we had something special."

"You killed the woman I loved, Ixia." My eyes narrowed on her. I stifled that rage that began to rise like a tsunami inside me. "And the baby she carried. You might as well kill me now, because as soon as I am free of this box, I am going to show you exactly how I feel about you." I stepped forward, my hands clenched into fists, my jaw tight and my chest heaving with angry breaths.

"Oh, that was a very long time ago, Damian. Don't you think it's about time we moved past all of that? Just think of this predicament you're in. I am the only one who can set you free. I think now is exactly the time that you should remember your manners and start being nice to me." She seemed extremely pleased with herself. I ground my teeth.

"Anyway, you should be thanking me." She placed a hand on her hip. "I could just go to the Zol Council and tell them I have you. They would torture you extensively until you reveal everything you know about that nagual beast of yours and her mate. I really don't know how you get yourself into these messes, Damian. Really?"

Her eyes were bright with excitement. She loved having the upper hand. Loved flaunting her power and using it to make others feel small and less significant.

"Fuck!" I roared. I just couldn't think past the rage that stung in my chest. I couldn't clear my thoughts enough to find a way out of here. I kicked the chair. It shook from the blow but didn't break. I raised my eyes to the ceiling and exhaled with a groan.

"I can see you're upset. You just need some time to cool down so I'm going to go. But before I do, I just want to leave you with this. I'm in a position to help you. In fact, I'm the only person in Zol Stria who can help you, and I believe we can help each other. But first you need some time to realize that you should be *thanking me*. Once you come to your senses, we'll talk. For now, just"—Ixia waved her hands in the air dismissively—"meditate or something."

It wasn't the cell that bothered me. It wasn't even the fact that I was trapped in here. The only thing that boiled my blood was that this bitch was still talking.

She left in a huff and I barely noticed. I ran my hands through my hair and paced my cell, wondering what the fuck I was going to do.

CHAPTER 22

This was a smothering kind of sadness. One that gripped my soul with an iron fist. One that squeezed at a deep and constant agony and fed it. One after another, the thoughts came barging in, never letting me breathe. I remembered Jenna's face as the sword was raised to her neck. Golden fire shown defiantly in her eyes, her lips in a straight, pursed line. She did not budge an inch. She did not reveal one hint of fear. The blade sliced and her blood splayed on the platform, and her beautiful existence met its end.

Over and over I recalled the deaths of each of my nagual unit in painstaking detail. I remembered the way the wind blew each hair on Bjorn's ginger beard before his last breath. The glare in Axel's eyes. Lex's stiff shoulders. Andres's spit on the ground. And Damian's torturous yell as the demon tore into him. It flooded my mind, rendering me useless as I remained there on the couch. I never once got up to eat or drink in the hours or days that followed.

Finally, my mouth was too dry and my legs demanded I stretch them. I sat up and managed to get a drink from the sink. When my eyes lifted to the window over the sink, I looked out upon a snowy winter. It was just summer. How could it be winter again? And that was when I noticed that these were my first thoughts of anything other than the deaths of my family.

I breathed in and thought about the beauty of the blanket of white that covered the ground and wondered how so much beauty could exist in a world where my family wasn't. I splashed water on my face. How could I move on without them? I looked in the mirror for answers and discovered my face had aged. I had gray hair and wrinkles and a scar where the Zolari Demon had sliced me.

What had happened to me? It didn't matter. I didn't matter.

I trudged back to the living room then opened the front door. Snow poured inside. The crisp air tingled against my skin so I put on the jacket, gloves and boots I found in the entryway. I would go for a walk.

I must have walked for hours. I wandered in one direction, then another. I couldn't see the sun, so I had no idea what time of day it was, but I just kept walking. I was in no rush to get anywhere anyway. A little creek came into view, now iced over. The snow was soft under my feet as I approached it. Frozen leaves cracked as I stepped on them. I followed that creek toward something I remembered other than the pain and sorrow of my life.

The creek expanded to a river. The Aries River. I remembered this, yes. It ran through the city of Venis where Aries Academy was. My eyes were all out of tears, otherwise they would be spilling down at the thought of the place where my family had been made. As I got closer to the town, a child approached me. Ash covered his small face and his clothes were ragged and torn.

The child opened his hands. He must have been hungry.

"I'm sorry, I don't have anything." My voice sounded raspy. Tired. Old. I took another step forward and my foot caught on a snow-covered rock. I slipped and the child moved in next to me, wrapping an arm around my waist.

"You need something to hold on to," the child said in a sweet, soft voice. He ran away and found a stick which he brought back to me. I used it to anchor myself. My bones were aching and I wasn't agile. I felt weak and very tired.

"I need to sit down," I told the child, and he brought me over to a nearby boulder.

We sat there for a while. A cold wind blew leaves off trees. The city of Venis was just a few feet away, over the bridge. Terrible memories plagued that city. It was empty now; I couldn't see any movement.

"Does anyone live there?" My voice cracked when I spoke.

"No one," the child said. "I've been waiting for you."

Slowly, I turned to look at the boy again. Black, messy hair covered his head. Equally dark eyes were wide and round. He reminded me of someone I knew very well.

"Why?" was all I could answer. I was still trying to understand who he was and why he was here.

"Because you needed me," he said, smiling. "Now, are you ready to walk some more?"

I nodded and got up slowly. My joints protested but I went along with him anyway.

We trudged into the city, me with my cane and the boy running eagerly ahead, picking up sticks or stones and inspecting them, then returning to my side. We passed a boutique with a mirror in the display window. I caught my reflection and approached it. My face was covered in wrinkles. My hair was completely white. I was an old woman. My entire life had gone by and I had been locked in a pit of sadness for all of it.

Regret washed over me. Regret for the life I hadn't lived because I'd let suffering keep me frozen in that little cabin in the woods. There were no more tears left to cry.

"Come on," the boy said. When I shifted my gaze to him, he seemed bigger somehow. He may have been eight when he'd first approached me, now he looked ten. I blinked, unsure of what was happening but too sad to care.

I followed him, too unsure of myself to do anything else.

"There. You'll find it there." He pointed toward the exact corner of the street where Damian had been attacked by that demon. My hands started to shake. Damian's blood was on my hands. Just like all the others.

"I've got to go now," the boy said.

Slowly, because I couldn't move quickly anymore, I panned my eyes back to him and watched as he ran off back to the woods where I'd found him.

My legs plodded toward the area where Damian had fallen. I stood there for a while without knowing what to do. My eyes landed on a black leather string on the sidewalk, poking out from under a bundle of frozen leaves. As I approached the string, the pile of leaves began to glow. I moved the leaves aside with my cane, revealing a glowing white stone on a black necklace.

"Now that looks familiar," I said out loud to no one at all.

I took off my gloves and used the cane to lift the interesting-looking necklace and wrapped it in my hands. The moment the warmth from the stone touched my skin, the emptiness in my heart began to fill. I felt a different kind of squeezing in my chest, one that held back the pain and filled my Zol with that old, familiar feeling of happiness. It was the most powerful emotion I had ever felt. It was love.

Find something to hold on to.

I squeezed the moonstone tighter and remembered him. I remembered the love I felt for Balastar. That inexplicable love that saturated my soul in the most delicious way whenever he was around. It rose in me like a tide and washed away my suffering.

I need to get back to him!

Like a river, the memory of what I was doing here in this world returned. I was on a trial in the phases of the moon. This was not real. None of this was fucking real. I slipped the necklace back over my neck and looked at my hands. They were still wrinkled. I took my long hair in my hands and saw that it was still white. Love gripped me tighter then. Love was the answer. I could suffer for the pain of those I'd lost, but I couldn't forget the love that had brought us together. I couldn't forget the love I had left to give in this world.

The buildings in front of me began to fade and I was in the blank white space that started this all. I had returned to the realm of the moon goddess Awilix.

My eyes landed on her. The wind blew in her hair and shadows swirled around her. She studied me carefully, her eyebrows pinched, then she relaxed them.

"You are the first to have passed the trials," she said, her voice a vast echo in this endless white space. "So many have failed where you have succeeded."

"How many?" I had to know.

"Two hundred and twenty-three over the course of one thousand years. I have many in my debt for the shadows are a gift I don't give lightly. But because of the strength of the love in your heart, you have earned the freedom of your kind from the death gods." Her voice reverberated around me.

"My kind, the nagual that live, and those that have yet to be born?"

"Yes."

"And none of that back there was real? I mean, my nagual family is still alive? Damian is still alive?" My voice broke. I couldn't keep the fear of that experience from shaking me to the core.

"It was very real. That is why these trials have been impossible to pass, until now. The trials occur in a reality parallel to your own world. They are simply alternate realities to the world you will return to now. Any of these realities could exist in any universe. But the past is gone, and the present of the moon trial you just experienced is now a thing of the past. And as for the future, well, that remains to be seen." As the words left her mouth, a chill raced down my spine.

She reached for my hand and gripped it with an unexpected kindness. And I believe I also saw respect in her eyes.

"How long was I gone?" I asked, staring at her soft hands around my frail, pale fingers.

She didn't answer me, but at her touch, my bones no longer ached. My hair returned to black. The wrinkles faded from my skin. I reached my fingers up to my face and felt for the scar. It was still there and that didn't matter to me.

I was still the Sasha Moreno I remembered, and I was finally free.

Chapter 23

Vucub-Cane's palace was strangely silent and, for a moment, I wondered if I was still part of the moon goddess's strange, parallel world. I searched the endless obsidian corridors and couldn't find anyone.

"Balastar?" I called. Then I called for Jenna and Lex. Bjorn and Axel. Andres and Eliana. No one answered me.

I continued up the stairs and headed to the room I shared with Balastar. His clean, citrus-and-oak scent filled my lungs, but it was mild. He hadn't been there in the past few days. I moved to the balcony that faced the lands where the armies had placed their camps. There were no signs of the armies at all, just a few stray dogs. Black ravens cawed and picked at the ground. But the Fae could not be seen.

What happened here and where is everyone?

My mind raced and my chest pounded. There was the scuffle of feet somewhere outside the bedroom. I hurried toward it, eager to hug my nagual family again, crazy with the urge to punch Bjorn on his massive bicep just so he can wink at me and shoo me away.

At the end of the hall, I found Dimitri, one of the Demon servants of the castle.

"Hi. Oh hey," I called to him from down the hall.

He stopped what he was doing and turned to me. "My... queen?" His face looked shocked, then a smile replaced his gaping mouth. "My queen! You've returned. What wonderful news. What wonderful news indeed." He dropped the tools he was holding and hurried over to me.

"Where is everyone?" I asked.

"They are at war..." His voice trailed off as though trying to figure out where to start. "The UnZol King was waiting for your return, but after a few weeks, he gave the orders."

"How long have I been gone?"

"I believe it's been a month now, my queen," he said.

I was gone a whole month! That was an entire moon cycle. I would have to contemplate the physics of that experience some other time. Right now, I had a war to fight.

Balastar, where are you? I sent a message down the bond and felt the connection to him thrum with life.

Sasha. There you are. Thank Zol. Wait for me there.

A few long hours passed before I finally heard footsteps shuffling from outside my room. I ran toward the sound.

"Jenna?" My heart thundered in my chest at the sight of her alive. The memory of her death was still fresh in my mind. Silent tears filled my eyes.

"Oh thank god, Sash. Come here bestie." She pulled me in for a massive hug. I shuddered in her arms, gripping her so tight for fear she would disappear. She must've Shadow Wove here from somewhere out there. All of my nagual unit had focused on cultivating this skill ever since our troubles at the Zodiac Prison.

"Are you ok? Hey... I'm right here. I'm not going anywhere." Her voice was tender and she pulled away to study my face.

"Yes." I sniffed. "Yes, I'm much better now. It was just so, real."

"Was it? Your moon trials were all anyone could talk about. They were all sure you were dead. If it wasn't for Balastar's connection to you, I would have believed them, too. But somehow, he knew you were alive. He just kept saying that you were lost." She smiled gently.

"I was very lost, in fact."

"You've got a nasty scar." She studied my face a bit more. "And I'm gonna be honest, you look very pale. I've never seen you like this." Her voice was full of concern.

"What do you mean?" I walked over to the mirror on top of my vanity. My eyes looked sunken in as though I hadn't slept in months. My skin was pasty and so pale you could see the blue veins clearly under it. My hair also looked like it hadn't been brushed in who knew how long. I smelled just as bad as I looked, too. I told Jenna I would jump in the shower and make myself more presentable. When I got out, Dimitri was standing next to the table on the balcony where an arrangement of food was displayed.

"I thought you might be hungry," Dimitri said.

"You know, I can't remember the last time I ate actual food. Thank you, Dimitri."

I immediately helped myself, and the taste of it all came to life in my mouth. I didn't even realize how hungry I was until the soft breads and cheeses covered my taste buds.

Jenna just sat back and watched. "Enjoy. I ate before coming, don't worry about me," she said after I lifted my eyes, embarrassed by the fact that I was just grabbing at everything.

Once I took the edge off my hunger, I began to wonder about everyone. Especially Damian. I was still in a fog after what happened in the Moon Ward. Everything had been so real; I needed to know he was ok. I scanned the room, expecting Balastar to be here by now. I wanted to thank him for the moonstone, for being my anchor.

"Where is Balastar? Why didn't he come?"

"He's in the middle of a negotiation with House Aries. I was with him before coming here. He asked me to be your proxy while he was gone, because he knew you trusted me." She searched my eyes, and I guessed she wanted to be sure I was ok with that. I was too drained of emotion to have much of a reaction so I simply nodded my head in approval.

"As soon as he heard you, he wanted to come," she continued. "He almost left, but they were about to send weapons of mass destruction through the tears in the Underworld. I convinced him to stay and finish his negotiation for the sake of all of us. Then I left to come here. The rest of the unit and the other nagual are there with him, guarding the rips in the wards of the Underworld." She waved her hand toward the far end of the valley at the edge of the Underworld.

"Is Aries really negotiating with us? I guess that's a step in the right direction. Tell me everything that's happened since I was gone," I managed to say between sips of the mango smoothie Dimitri had brought me.

"Well, then let me start with the fact that your man is truly ruthless. I mean, now I know where he gets his fame as the Dark King. About two weeks ago he sensed something was wrong with you. That was around the same time Damian went missing—"

My eyes opened wide. "Wait, what? Damian's missing?"

"You eat. Just let me tell the story, ok? Ask questions after." She pursed her lips and pointed at the food. I took another bite of the baguette with fig jam.

"Damian was captured by Ixia when he went on an unauthorized mission into Zol Stria. Luckily Vera followed him and she came back here to tell us where he was. That was about the same time when Balastar convinced the generals to launch the first wave of attacks. I had no idea he had legions of UnZol soldiers waiting dormant right underneath the cities. He unleashed them on Aries and Capricorn, because those were the two Houses that were sending their forces through those tears.

"The thing is, those UnZol soldiers are the undead of the legends. They literally don't have Zols at all. Their skin is like white rubber, their eyes and blood are black, and they have these obscenely large, white fangs. They attack in herds and it's been brutal. That's how they've gotten past the elemental magic of the Zol Council."

"I'm not sure how I feel about this," I said, setting down the apple I was eating. "I had some idea he commanded forces like that. He told me that in the old wars he'd controlled the armies of the Zolless. But that he knew it would be dangerous to unleash them again because they can be a threat to civilians. Why would he do this now?"

"Well, the Council was breaking through the tears in the Underworld. They had already killed at least a thousand of our soldiers and, if left unchecked, they would have cornered us down here. We were essentially being trapped inside. We needed a way to attack from the outside." Her jade eyes were sharp and focused.

"Remember? That was our mission once you freed us from the bond to the death gods," she said. "But you took so long, and things were getting ugly here. And we began to worry that you may never come back. The idea that you would pass the moon trials began to seem impossible to many of the nagual that didn't know you." She shook her head. "But I knew you would come back to us. I could feel it. And the moment you returned I felt this huge weight lift from my shoulders. I felt lighter somehow. You did it, didn't you? The mission worked?" She smiled hopefully, squeezing my hand. I squeezed hers in return.

"Yes, it worked." I wanted to sound excited, but I wasn't ready. I was still mourning her death and the death of all the others, though they didn't really happen. I was still in shock from the decades I'd spent in the Moon Ward, reliving their deaths and blaming myself for them every day and every night. Even though Jenna was right there in front of me, I couldn't just shake off the pain of losing her like it had never happened. I reached for her and wrapped my arms around her warm body. She returned my embrace and I released my tears into her shoulder, crying like I had never cried before in my life. Jenna rubbed my back patiently, lovingly.

"It's ok now. You're home. Whatever you went through in there, it's over. You did it. You did the impossible Sasha. You are safe now," she said in a soft, compassionate voice. She held me there until I stopped sobbing and brought me tissues to wipe my tears.

I leaned back in my chair and smiled at her. "I sure as shit returned. I'm not going to let you guys have all the glory of taking down the Council." I chuckled as I dabbed my eyes one last time.

"It's like the truth was right in front of us about the Zol Council the whole time we were in the Academy, but we just didn't see it," she said.

"Well, now we can go wherever the fuck we want without anyone controlling us. We are just as free as the next Fae." My eyes were heavy and my body began to feel the weight of the past month. I was completely depleted.

"Thank you, Sash. What you did for us will never be forgotten," a gruff voice said from the doorway.

"Bjorn!" I forgot my weariness and raced for him. My arms squeezed tight around his waist. He lifted me in the air like I was nothing but a doll and spun me around.

Axel, Lex, Andres and Eliana spilled into the room to greet me, bursting with relief and happiness. I hugged them one by one for longer than any of them expected and couldn't decide who to hear from first. Then I told them everything I could about what had happened to me while in the Moon Ward.

After a while, I was sitting on the couch next to Bjorn while Axel and he were talking about the squad of Nightwalkers that had attacked their tent in the middle of the night.

His voice began to fade into the background as my eyes shut. With my hair still damp from my shower, my belly full, and surrounded by almost everyone I loved the most in this world, I leaned my head on Bjorn's warm, firm arm and fell into a deep, restful sleep.

CHAPTER 24

Somehow, I made it to my bed and awoke to a bright light from the tiny suns streaming in through the slit between the curtains. My heart began to pound in my chest when I opened my eyes.

Damian is missing. Balastar has released the Zolless armies. What am I doing sleeping in this late?

I sat up in a bit of a panic.

"Hey, calm down, you'll give yourself a heart attack," Balastar said.

I snapped my head to where he was sitting in a comfortable armchair next to my bed. His face was half covered in shadows.

"Oh, what are you doing here?" I was still sleepy and confused.

"Watching you rest."

I wiped a few stray hairs off my face and wet my lips, hoping I didn't look like a complete wreck in front of this stupidly gorgeous man. "How long have I been sleeping?"

"At least a day." He smiled. Somehow that pleased him.

"I'm famished." My stomach growled as though it had just awoken, too. "But we don't have time to eat. I've got to find a way to get to Damian. We've got to shadow weave into the Great Houses. This war has to end." I threw off the blanket and slid my legs off the bed.

Balastar stood up and planted himself right in front of me.

"Trust me, there will be time for all of that. First, you should eat." He motioned toward the tray of food. There were fresh croissants, butters and jams, bananas and apples. I ate a healthy serving while he brought me up to speed on the war effort, then I freshened up in the bathroom.

"We agreed to let you sleep because of the state you were in. While you were in the trials, I demanded to see Awilix, and finally got a meeting through Vucub-Cane. She told us the extent of your trials and I almost lost it on her." He shook his head in frustration.

"Your mind had been twisted and turned every which way for a whole moon phase and you didn't even know it. It was by the grace of Zol you even survived out there. Everything that happened to you was as real as what is happening right now." His eyes seemed distant, all too aware of what that meant.

"Like this scar is real." I raised my fingers to my face and traced it.

"Yes, exactly like that. And for the record, you make scars look beautiful," he said.

I smiled and flung myself back on the bed. "Was it like that in the Void?"

"I can't say for sure, because I haven't been to the Moon Ward. All I know is what I've read in the archives and the stories shared among my people. I can tell you that the Void was both everything and nothing. So if I were to guess, yes, in some ways it was like the Moon Ward." His eyes darkened. "The Void is a place of perpetual, endless suffering. From what I know about the Moon Ward, the Void is different from the Moon Ward because I could witness this realm and not be part of it." His eyes turned downward and he seemed completely broken for the briefest heartbeat, then he was back to the composed Balastar I knew.

He returned his gaze to meet mine. "Worst of all, I could witness all that was happening to you and not do anything about it."

I reached for him. His hand was warm to my touch. "Come sit with me."

Balastar got up from the chair and joined me on the bed. He pulled me closer to him and I released a deep, shaky sigh.

"What else did you see? What else happened to you?" I asked.

"I can't put it in words. I can't explain the hundreds of years watching, forgetting, then remembering. Being pulled then released. Ripped apart and renewed. Over and over again. At a certain point, you become numb to it all. You become like a floating piece of wood down a river, only you can sense and feel everything and every emotion is torn to shreds." Dark clouds covered his eyes.

"After years of this kind of floating, I became numb to the worst of it. Until the moment you returned to the world. The very day you were born I could sense your presence. Only I hid my happiness. I buried it deep so nothing within that Void could discover my emotion and prey upon it. It was the only way they wouldn't find you. I watched and I waited. When I could, I fought the demons that hunted you before your transition. Because I hid my true feelings, I was able to keep those demons at bay. I could never let on as to why I was protecting you. I helped open the channel for Zayne to come through and guide you to finding Damian." He swept a hand through my hair so tenderly that my voice caught in my throat.

"You were there for me." The realization that I wasn't alone, even back then when I'd been so lost and afraid of everything happening to me, brought warmth to my chest.

"In this life and the next. I will always be there for you."

This was the man I needed. The man I wanted. I leaned into him and traced his jaw with my fingers. His eyes met mine and lingered there, searching them as I searched his. Within those dark pools I could see the depths of the same kind of darkness that I commanded.

"There's something about your eyes that I don't understand. How do they change shape like that?"

He blinked a few times, a side of his mouth tugging upward. "They weren't always like that, you know. It's the only thing about me that's changed after I came back from the Void. Oh, and the tattoos on my back."

"It's like the Zodiac Shadows are inside your eyes. Like they have their own mind. Maybe you have some new abilities because of it." I stretched myself up to place my lips on each of his eyes and then his mouth. Then I lifted his shirt and traced my fingers along the ancient scripture tattooed down the middle of his back, letting my lips meet the black lines I found there.

When I finished, he gripped me, pulling me into his embrace. His intoxicating scent danced over my skin, sliding through it and lighting fire to my desire for him.

He reached his hand down to my thigh and gripped me just as heat began to rise from my center and started to burn. His lips met mine and his tongue glided over my teeth; my tongue searched for his. A growl reverberated in his throat as he advanced his hands around my waist and back, pulling me even closer toward him as his lips dragged down to my jaw then my neck. I scrambled to touch him, to feel his firm muscles against my fingers. Felt his hard, expanding steel in my palm as I rubbed against him. A desperate moan left my throat as the desire for him continued to grow and grow.

I lifted myself on top of him, straddling him as he sat on the side of the bed. He lifted my nightgown over my head, casting it aside as he soaked me in with his eyes. I took several long breaths as he gazed at me with those mesmerizing dark eyes. He had no idea how terribly frantic I was in my need of him. A need that was begging to be released.

He reached his hand up to my jaw and ran his thumb over my lips. I slipped it into my mouth, wetting it with my tongue and wrapping my lips around it. He bit his lower lip as I grazed his skin with my teeth. Slowly, he removed his thumb and gripped my breast, lowering his mouth as his heated breath made me arch my back. He caught my nipple in his mouth, his tongue working around the top and driving me to the height of pleasure.

My head flung back as a low, sultry moan escaped my lips. He continued to work magic with his tongue down the center of my chest and waist as I rolled onto my back on the bed. His lips met my center and wetness awaited him. My body responded to every touch, moving in time with him in a fit of sensual pleasure. He was lighting me on fire with every flick of his tongue. My fire element rose to my fingers, and I lifted my palms.

"I feel the heat from you. You are so fucking hot," he said, lifting his head. His eyes panned to the fire that rose from my hands and reached for me, pulling my hand toward him. He brought his lips through the fire and kissed my palm. The flames had no effect on him. They skipped across his face and made him glow, but they didn't burn him.

"What?" I panted, my arousal still peaking. "How is that possible?"

"One of the benefits of being a demigod." He smiled. He moved to the center of the bed, bringing me with him and exploring me again with his hands.

I did some exploring of my own. The lines of his muscles were firm and hard. The cuts of his stomach awakened some primitive need to feel them against my lips and tongue. He was responding to my touch now, growling low and steady.

I played with his body for a while, feeling every part of him. My damp lips on his cock, the length of him surprising me once again. I was in control of his passion, of his sensuality, and I liked being in control. The Dark King was giving himself to me, and just the thought of that filled me with my own sense of power.

Dark tendrils of my shadow mist sprung to life all around me. Curling around his arms, twining around mine. It was our dark magic that wanted to intertwine. The sensation of my shadows combining with his filled a deep, broken longing in my chest. It electrified my senses, and a profound wisdom within me knew that he was making me stronger.

I positioned myself over him, and he focused his eyes on me as his hands gripped my waist. He slid into me, filling my center as my wetness pooled over him, hot and simmering. Balastar and I rocked, steady and strong, over and over until my pleasure erupted. I screamed in rapture, and he moaned in response.

I collapsed on him. My breath came in pants as my muscles relaxed. I ran my hands softly across his chest and arms. Feeling the light sheen of sweat that had formed on his flesh disappear made me think how truly amazing it was that we were together again.

After we lay in a peaceful silence, I got up.

"Where are you going?" He gripped my arm, keeping me next to him.

"We have so much to do. There's a war to fight and we have to get Damian. I would love to lay here all day, but time is of the essence." He released his grip and instead softly caressed my back. I began to shift again.

"This is true... One more time before we go? It will be faster this time, I promise." The warmth of his lips still lingered on me and my body grew excited with the idea of feeling him all over again.

"Really fast," I said, feeling guilty for taking the time for this.

"Yes, really fast," he breathed in my ear.

"And right after we go lead this war."

"Yes, right after."

I began to feel less guilty now that his hands were once again warming my flesh.

"Ok," I agreed, and he kept his promise.

CHAPTER 25

The devastation of the beautiful city of Venis was heartbreaking. I knew the festive, happy people who'd made their homes and businesses here. My heart felt heavy in my chest as I surveyed the broken walls, the black soot that covered everything and the bricks and broken things that littered the ancient cobblestone streets.

Jenna, Lex and Balastar's closest general had joined us on this mission. I was anxious to see firsthand what was going on from ground level. We were also accompanied by three Arcana Angels of the Underworld. In a few moments we would have an informal meeting with one of Zol Stria's ambassadors to gauge Zol Stria's position.

The destruction before me made it difficult to speak.

"I wanted our freedom, but I didn't want this." Remorse laced my words.

"No one ever wants this," Balastar replied somberly.

"Where is everyone? What happened to the people who lived here?" I asked Balastar, as I tried not to imagine the panic the people that lived hear must of felt as their city was destroyed.

Just then, within one of the broken homes, I heard shuffling and picked up the scent of a young Fae and his mother.

"They need our help." I could also tell by the scent that one of them was bleeding.

We entered the crumbling home and found a mother and child huddled up in a corner. Natives, from the look of it, for the Fae of this city had distinctive black hair, bright blue eyes and blue wings. Unlike the Arcana Angels who could fly, their wings were only suited for gliding.

Just as we could identify her, the mother knew us by our black battle gear and symbol of the Underworld. She shuddered and crouched away in fear.

"Please. Please don't hurt us," she begged, her eyes open wide. My eyes shot to her son; he was about thirteen or fourteen, his wings not yet fully grown. The mother appeared to be applying pressure to one of them, probably staunching some bleeding.

"We aren't here to hurt you. We're here to help," I replied.

Just then, one of the Arcana Angels landed outside the entryway. His voice was urgent. "The ambassador is approaching. He has about six militia with him; they're all on horseback."

Balastar caught my questioning look. "You're wondering why they didn't show up in cars?"

"Yes, I am," I said.

"We agreed to have diplomatic meetings on horseback. That way there wouldn't be any hidden passengers or weapons larger than one could carry on them," he explained.

"Got it," I replied, turning to the mother. "Will you let us help you?"

The mother looked at her son, who was pale from blood loss. She hesitated, then nodded slowly.

"Jenna, send for a healer for this woman's son. Fast."

"Yes, my queen," Jenna said.

I gently wrapped my hand around Jenna's arm and walked her outside.

"If that kid doesn't get help soon, he will lose his wings permanently. He may even die from the blood loss."

"I saw that." Her eyes darted back inside the house where the mother waited with her child, then focused back on me. "I'm on it," she said and shadow wove away.

The ambassador was Elris Estevan and I knew him from our time together in the Academy. He was the Vicar of House Aries, born into wealth and status, and not very ambitious. Elris skated by in life, had everything handed to him, and never had to work hard to gain wealth or influence.

"Hello, Elris," I said as he dismounted his horse.

"Greetings, everyone. Let's make this quick, shall we? Call off your forces and we won't kill every last one of you. That's our deal." He'd gained weight since the last time I'd seen him as he fumbled with the horse reins as he threw them over the saddle.

"Was it a pleasant ride over? I didn't know you were one to ride horses," Balastar said casually.

He scoffed. "The ride over was lovely, thank you very much. Now let's get on with this."

Balastar took a step forward and Elris took a step back, eyes opening wide and mouth rounding at the corners. "We are not here to negotiate. We will only negotiate with the King of House Aries. Where is he?"

"Oh, he's not coming. You'll have to negotiate with me."

Fire burned in Balastar's eyes. His anger paused as Jenna arrived with a healer. She scurried her inside to attend to the child and I breathed a sigh of relief.

"What was that? What's going on there?" Elris asked, his voice quivering slightly.

"Nothing. Just a mother who needed care for her child. What happened to the people of this cityvillage? Where are they all?" I asked.

Elris relaxed his shoulders and smirked. "She doesn't know?" he asked Balastar.

Balastar's eyes darkened.

"Your people did this. Your UnZol army came through and destroyed everything. They killed everyone. This is why my king won't meet you. This is why I came. No one else wants to negotiate. You're all monsters."

I fought the urge to gape at Balastar. Instead, I kept my face cold and unreadable.

He continued, "The other eleven Houses have rallied behind Aries. They are ready to attack and finish this once and for all. But many people will die on both sides. I suggest you call them off and surrender."

"We will do no such thing. This war will end when the Zol Council accepts our conditions, stops their oppression of our people and grants us equal voting rights in each of the Houses. It's quite simple really. Otherwise, each of the Houses will fall," Balastar said.

Elris began to mount his horse. His movements were laborious and slow but he managed to scoot up into the saddle without falling.

"We'll never agree to those conditions," he spat, spittle flying from his mouth.

CHAPTER 26

The Fae woman and her child emerged from the home. The boy's bleeding had stopped and some color had returned to his face. The mother's face was less worried as she held on to his arm as he walked. The healer emerged shortly after. When the mother looked toward Elris and his small militia, her eyes lit brightly.

"Sir. Sir, please help us. We need your help." She approached his horse but he turned away, ignoring her. "Sir, we are your people. You must help us!"

He kicked at his horse and the militia began walking in the direction from where they'd come. She kept up with them as they got farther away from us. Balastar and Jenna turned their attention away from the departing group of militia and they began talking amongst themselves. I kept my eye on the woman, and watched as she ran up to one of the armed men with her son in tow. She reached for his cloak and when he shrugged her off, the boy began yelling at his mother to stop but she continued. But she grabbed at another male, sobbing and demanding that they take her and the child with them.

One of the cloaked soldiers stopped his horse and jumped off it. He slapped her with the back of his hand and she fell to the ground with a whimper.

I hurried forward, yelling, "Hey, not cool. Are you ok?"

She ignored me.

"I can't help you," the soldier said in a low voice. "The caravans have all left, and they won't be returning."

"Fuck you," she spat out as he turned away. "I hope you lose the war, you heartless bastards!" The woman raised her hand to her face where the soldier had slapped her and, before I got close enough to stop it, the soldier removed his knife and slit her throat in one cold stroke. The kid yelled and flared his wounded wings as he charged for the soldier. The soldier was about to slice at him when I surrounded the kid with a shadow shield.

"You come here to blame us for the harm done to your people, then you kill her?" I yelled loud enough for Elris to hear as he rode away. My fire element rose to the surface and my jaguar clawed at me from the inside, begging to be released on him.

"She had it coming," the soldier grunted as he wiped his blade clean on his pant leg.

"These are clearly your people. She went to you for help, not us!" I snarled, ready to release my jaguar on him. Instead, I released the fire.

A blaze of orange heat cast from my palms set Elris and his entourage stumbling backward. Jenna raised air and Lex created a rift in the earth to separate the militia from us. Balastar had given us explicit instructions not to kill them. Killing an ambassador or his militia escort during a diplomatic meeting would go against the conventions and lead to far greater problems negotiating with the Houses in the long run.

I hissed my now-extended jaguar fangs at the militia, the need for a taste of their blood ever present on my tongue.

The boy stumbled backward, trying to avoid the rift in the earth as he dragged his mother's body away from it. He knelt at her side, holding her hand in both of his.

I threw up my hands. "There's no negotiating with them."

"We've got to get out of here before the Zolless return." Balastar's eyes were focused on something behind us; a gray mist had begun to loom in the distance.

"Is that them?" I asked.

"Yes," he said.

"And they did all this?"

Darkness hooded his eyes as he replied, "Yes."

I loved him with all my Zol, but I wasn't about to allow myself to be blinded by this.

"How could you do this, Balastar? All of these people? You've got to find a way to contain them. You've got to stop this! Right now," I pleaded.

He refused to yield. "It is the only way. We all would have died down there. We'd never win this war otherwise. This is our chance to get everything we want. We need to hold out."

"We need to protect the civilians. Surely there's some form of magic, some way to contain the Zolless inside a ward until we need them. They can't be allowed to just wander free and kill whomever they wish. I'm not having it. You've got to stop it." My rage was rising as hot as burning coals within my chest and in my palms. I looked to Jenna, who was kneeling on the ground, comforting the kid. Then I scanned to Lex, who grimaced at the scene before him.

I was furious with Balastar for releasing those troops. It was, in my eyes, yet another betrayal. I gave the signal to Lex, one that we'd cultivated in our years of training together. It was a signal that I was going to shadow weave away. He shook his head and I stopped pulling in the shadows. I was frozen and not because anyone had tried to stop me, but because I couldn't figure out what to do.

"Fuck!" I screamed and stormed toward the buildings.

"Lex, look after the boy. Balastar..." Jenna held out a hand to him, motioning him to stay where he was and not approach me. "Let me talk to her."

Jenna ran up to me. "What are you doing?"

"I want to leave. I want to get the fuck away from that... monster. I'm so pissed at him," I hissed through my teeth.

"No, Sasha. That was a disaster the last time, remember? You can't keep running away when shit gets hard. You have to face him head-on."

I stopped in my tracks and tried to wrestle with what she was saying. *She's right. I'm trying to run away again.*

All those years ago, when I joined the military after my trouble back home, I was running from my demons. Then, when I found out Trent was fucking Solana, I ran into the forest and got myself captured and thrown in the Zodiac prison. Now that I didn't like what Balastar was doing with his armies, I was trying to run away again.

I released a heavy sigh.

"You're right." My chest began to cool and my palms released the fire just beneath their surface. I shifted my gaze to Balastar, who was speaking with his general but looking over at me. When my eyes met his, I caught his expression. He didn't want me to leave.

"Fine. I won't leave," I growled to Jenna, "but I can't even talk to him now. I just can't understand how this was the only solution. How we couldn't have come up with a better way to handle this? The plan was to wait for me to get the nagual released from the death gods so we could shadow weave in and take out the Council. That was the whole point. The plan was never this. I can't see how this is forgivable, Jenna."

Jenna placed a hand on my shoulder. Her beautiful, dark skin, green eyes and golden hair were a familiar comfort. "Listen, this is war and not every decision will be the right one. We were all there when he decided to send in the Zolless. The nagual agreed to his plan. So if you're upset, you're going to have to be upset at us, too. We sent warnings to the civilians before they attacked. Some of them listened and headed to the safe zones we secured for them. But most of them decided not to evacuate. They decided to stay because they thought this was a trap, while others thought it was all a lie just to take control of the city."

I sighed in a relief that some effort had been made to protect the people. I uncrossed my arms. "Well, at least there's that."

"And maybe now the other Houses will take this as a warning of what could happen to them," she said.

I nodded in agreement, then changed my mind. "No, Jenna, we can never use the Zolless armies again. They are too destructive. *We* are the answer. The nagual will go in and finish this."

"Ok then. Go tell your man." She tilted her head in his direction.

"Fine. I will. And I'm going to make sure he has some sort of plan to rein in the Zolless that are now on the loose."

I still hadn't forgiven him, but a part of me could understand why he did what he had. I decided then that I would forgive him, eventually.

CHAPTER 27

DAMIAN

I scratched at my groomed beard as I sat in the chamber that Ixia had trapped me in. Over the past two weeks I'd had a chance to calm down and think things through a little differently. And with a calm mind, I opened up to new possibilities.

After almost five hundred years, Ixia knew me well. She knew I always smelled good and wore the finest clothes. Every day, she conjured a fresh set of clothes into my cell and replenished my grooming supplies in the bathroom. She also made sure I had plenty of my favorite foods and drinks appear on the small table. The chamber was also pretty comfortable with enough space to walk around. The armchair lay flat, which made it easy to get a decent night's rest. There were plenty of books to read and a television just outside the room that Guido controlled.

This was not the sign of a captor who wanted me to hate them. She wanted to win some favor with me and it was making me think that she hadn't told the rest of the Council I was in her custody. They would have stormed in by now and taken me as their own prisoner. Either to negotiate with the UnZol Army, or to kill as an example. She had hidden me here and now I needed to figure out why.

"Hey, Guido, let's see who's winning the smashball tournament," I said.

Guido looked up at me from his phone. He lifted a puffy hand for the remote and turned it on so we could watch. "The score's close," he grunted.

"Yeah," I said, concentrating on the television. I was glad Ixia had installed speakers in here so I could hear everything on the other side of the glass.

The main door opened and Ixia strolled in, her green dress fitted close and her long golden curls loose around her shoulders. Her dress was very short today. Her heels were extra high and her makeup was flawless. "Guido, go get a snack or something," she said as she approached the glass.

"Ok," he said gruffly as he lifted himself up slowly out of the armchair. When he was gone, Ixia began pacing in front of the glass. She hadn't stopped by in days.

She stopped pacing and studied me. "You seem calm now."

I nodded. "I am."

"Are you ready to tell me what the nagual are up to?" Her voice sounded urgent and worried.

"I've been in here for almost two weeks now. How am I supposed to know what they're up to?" I glanced from her to the television as if we were a couple having a casual conversation in my living room.

"Damian. I know you know something. They've killed four House monarchs already. The Kings of Scorpio, Libra and Aries, and just last night the Queen of House Aquarius. Killed by surprise with the mark of the jaguar. Hun-Cane has all but disappeared and rumor has it that he's not been able to stop them. That goes against the very laws of the nagual's existence. They've always been under the gods' control. The Council believes both the death gods are now favoring the Dark Zodiac. Is it true?" Although Ixia had a talent for keeping herself cool no matter what the situation, her voice hinted at desperation.

Yes! Sasha made it through the Moon Ward.

"From the sounds of it," I said, still casual, "they're going to after all the Houses. And once all the monarchs are down, they will kill the second-in-lines. Then the third. Then the fourth. Until everyone on the Council is dead." I returned my attention to the game.

She reached for the remote on the table and turned off the television. I raised my arms in protest. "The Blood Ravens were about to score!"

"Listen, Damian." Her voice had softened. "You need to tell me how they're doing that. How do they slip underneath Hun-Cane's watch? Ever since they began killing off the rulers, Hun-Cane can't be found. It's like even he knows there's nothing he can do about it."

Ixia placed a hand on her hip and looked away as if thinking about something else. Then she faced me again. "Just think of what we can be together. You and I, we can come in with the solution to stop all of this killing, all of this destruction. You just need to tell me what is going on."

I rose from the armchair and approached the glass. "You're going to need to be more specific, Ixia. How do I know that you'll actually let me out of here if I tell you anything?"

She smiled a slight, sultry smile. "Because I'll let you out now, before you tell me anything. And we can seal our truth in binding magic."

"Fine." I nodded. It would take all my years of masking my emotions to get me through what I would have to do next.

CHAPTER 28

There's nothing like the sunrise. I hadn't realized how much I'd missed it after spending so much time in the Underworld. The bright oranges and pinks were painted on the sky, and the water was a mirror of the sun's magnificent arrival.

"Isn't it amazing?" I said, my voice low and soft.

"Yeah, it really is," Jenna replied.

The King of Pisces' blood was still fresh on my hands as we looked out upon the ocean, just outside of the zodiac wheel we would be traveling through. In order to travel between the different Houses, we had to get to the zodiac wheel, which could only be navigated by the Zol Sen.

What we had in our favor was that the Zol Sen were impartial to the war efforts, including the Wheel Guides. They were the Zol Sen that operated the zodiac wheels. They remained neutral, uninfluenced by politics. To do otherwise would be to go against their nature and connection to the cosmos. No matter who was in power, the Zol Sen were only loyal to the stars. But that didn't keep Zol Stria from sending their own forces to stand watch at the wheels just in case.

Jenna and I surveyed the zodiac wheel we were about to go through.

"Something smells off," I said.

"Definitely," she agreed, eyes scanning the open doorway that led to the wheel that was kept at the Pisces marina.

"I'll go in and take a look through the shadows," I said.

She nodded.

I pulled dark energy into me and shadow wove into mist and darkness so that I could curl up and around the sides of the walls. I followed the scent as my shadows pulsed and thrummed, leading me back through the corridors to the room where the zodiac wheel was kept.

There, a Zol Sen had bled out on the floor.

The blood was fresh, so this murder had been recent. Even after all the blood I'd shed myself, I shuddered at the sight of the Zol Sen. They were sacred, untouchable Fae. No one would do such a thing, or so I'd always thought. I realized I was wrong.

We left the marina and shadow wove to the location of the next zodiac wheel, which was at City Hall and found another Wheel Guide dead on the floor. Then we made it to the third and final wheel at Pisces, only to find that Wheel Guide had met his fate as well.

"The Council must've found out about the deaths of the other leaders and killed the Zol Sen to keep us from getting out. Now how are we going to get back to Aries?" My heart began to race.

"We haven't checked the siren's zodiac wheel. The one at the bottom of the ocean," Jenna said.

"Yeah, good idea. With the number of sirens in this House, that one's got to be open." Each Gate had at least one zodiac wheel under water to accommodate the high population of sirens that lived there. We found the scuba gear we needed to get us down there on a yacht in the harbor.

"You don't really need your scuba gear down there, do you?" I asked Jenna, more out of curiosity about the extent of her air powers than anything else.

"No, not really, but Balastar had a vision about it. He said he saw something about us needing to be in the water but he wasn't sure why. He told me to have it prepared just in case." She shrugged.

One of Balastar's gifts was the sight. The Devil's Eye was one of the relics used to bring Balastar back from the Void, a relic that gave the holder a view past wards and into whatever they focused on. That included a limited view of the future.

When Balastar had returned from the Void, he'd held this same power. It was how we'd been able to identify where the rulers of the Houses would be at the moments we attacked them.

We'd found the King of House Scorpio in a brothel. Jenna and I had entered the room as his hired escorts, and I'd slit his throat as I stood behind his hairy and bloated body. In the kitchen, Jenna had slipped poison into the drink of the King of House Libra just before he'd had his dinner served to him.

The King of House Aries was hiding in a bunker when we came for him. Lex shadow wove into his quarters and the king fought hard for his life. The King of Aries was a trained warrior, but Lex won in the end, shifting into his jaguar form and piercing his neck from behind.

The Queen of House Aquarius was very young; she wasn't a strong warrior but she wanted to be. Axel killed her combat instructor so he could take his place in her training. He was in the middle of showing her how to free herself from a choke hold when he shifted and ripped her arteries out of her throat.

The King of House Pisces was as slippery as a wet fish. We found him outside in his garden, feeding the Koi in his pond. As soon as he got a whiff of us, he shifted into his siren form and jumped in the water. He was trying to get through an escape route he had at the far end of the pond, but I shifted into my jaguar form in mid-air as I leapt for him. I landed on his back and pressed him to the floor of the pond. He struggled under the weight of my jaguar and I yanked him out with my teeth. Jenna finished the job with a clean slice to his throat.

With our scuba gear on, we dove down to the bottom of the harbor and swam to the cave entrance of the zodiac wheel. Siren warriors were coming through, so we hid nearby and waited.

Shadow weaving in water was impossible; it was too difficult to draw in the dark energy we needed through physical matter. My fire element was also out of commission in the water, making our retreat much more difficult than any before it.

As Jenna and I waited for the sirens to pass, one of them slowed down. He had huge biceps, a massive chest and mid-section, and he would have been at least four feet taller than me if we were standing next to each other on land. His long red hair was tied back into a low ponytail and he wore the crest of the Council on his shoulder. It seemed he caught our scent. He descended on us like lightning.

There was no way we could outswim him, so we had to fight. He was in front of me before I realized what was happening and punched me right in the face. The mouthpiece was thrown from my lips and my mask broke. Jenna, who was a few yards behind me, used her air magic to shield me. Thank Zol she did because another three other sirens rushed to help the first.

They became stuck behind her air shield as she dragged me to the zodiac wheel. My lungs were tight and my face began to turn red.

I was drowning.

My eyes bulged as the salt water stung them. I tried to get Jenna's attention so she could give me her gear, but she didn't or couldn't notice. She kept her focus on getting me to the zodiac wheel. Behind us, the sirens thrashed hard against the air shield. *If only she could send some of that air my way!*

In my panic I began to suck in water, which stung as it filled my lungs. Frantically, I reached for Jenna's arm. She finally looked at me and her eyes opened wide. Still projecting the air shield, she released me and yanked out her mouthpiece. I took a deep, filling breath. Then another. Then a few more until I finally reached the deepest crevice of each lung and satisfied them with the air they needed. I tried to hand it back to her but she refused to take it, instead creating her own air bubble for breathing.

The moment both our feet were within the Aries Gate section of the zodiac wheel, the siren Zol Sen granted us passage.

As soon as we crossed the wheel to the other side, we arrived in Aries's underwater territory where Balastar had a small siren army waiting for us. They were dissenters of Council-ruled Zol Stria. The more we fought the Zol Council, the more supporters would appear and pledge their allegiance to us. They escorted us to Balastar's vessel on the surface where I choked and coughed out all the water that had creeped into my lungs.

"How did you know?" I coughed out.

"I used the sight from the Devil's Eye," he said as he covered me with a blanket. "That was too dangerous. I'm going with you next time."

I took my time to recover on the passage back to our command center in Aries Academy. When we arrived, he brought me into the library.

"I was finally able to find Damian with the sight," he said. "Ixia had him guarded with some kind of new ward I couldn't identify. I kept poking at it but it wouldn't budge. It looks like she released him from the ward now. But you won't believe what he's doing." Balastar shook his head.

"What? Tell me."

"He's about to rail her, like, right now."

I gaped at him.

"W-What?" I stammered.

"He's about to fuck her."

"That's absolutely insane." Was all I could manage to say.

What was Damian thinking?

CHAPTER 29

DAMIAN

I xia's plan had finally dawned on me. I was her safety net. Or, at least, one of her safety nets. She always had a few things going on at once. Ixia was always looking out for her own survival and kept herself a few steps ahead of the game.

She wasn't turning me in to the Council and was treating me well in here because she was beginning to realize she was on the losing side. Also, in case through some unexpected turn of events the Council won, she would be the one who had the information that could lead to capturing the nagual. And beyond all of that, she might even be holding on to some dream that she and I could be together.

She warded herself heavily when she let me out of the chamber, but she didn't call Guido back in. I tested her by extending out my own awareness, and it was met with a firm magical wall.

"How are we supposed to bind our magic if you've got all those wards up?" I scoffed.

She hesitated, then let the wards drop one layer at a time.

I reached my hand out to hers and she shook it, our magic intertwining and connecting.

"I promise not to kill you after you tell me the nagual's plan," she said.

The power of zodiac magic surged through us, sealing the promise.

We released our hands and I gazed into her eyes. I tried to remember those times where I'd felt more for her. I'd never truly loved her, and that had always been our issue. For over two hundred years while we were together, I was with her without loving her. However, she'd loved me fiercely. I left her, and while I slept with many other women, she seemed comforted in the fact that I never loved any of them, either. That was, until I met Sasha's aunt, Lily. I didn't know love could be so compelling, so demanding of my Zol.

And when Ixia realized my heart could love someone, just not her, it'd driven her mad. Mad enough to kill the woman I loved and the unborn child she was carrying.

Rage swelled within me for decades. There was so much rage that I couldn't function. I retreated into myself and ran away from the world.

Now here she was, the murderer of my greatest love, and I was going to kiss her. I reached one hand to her waist and pulled her toward me. Then I met her soft lips to mine. I searched her mouth with my tongue and felt her knees buckle. She gripped my arms, her fingers squeezing tightly, her mouth eager and full of longing.

She reached for me everywhere as though her hands had been anticipating this very moment. "Damian, I've missed you. I can't tell you how much I've missed you." Her breath was heavy and her chest heaved with each word.

"Ixia. I'm going to tell you everything," I whispered in her ear with heated breath. She reached for my shirt, pulling me close and meeting her lips to my neck and then my ear.

"The nagual are no longer under the control of the gods," I said. "Sasha transited the Moon Ward to release herself from Awilix's magic."

Ixia stopped kissing me and pulled herself back, releasing my shirt as if it'd burned her. "What? That makes them too powerful. Too deadly. There have never been any Fae, other than the UnZol King, to hold so much power."

"Now there are." I smiled at her. "The Zol Council will fall in a matter of days."

She tried to flee to the door, but I grabbed her. I wrapped my hands around her neck and started squeezing. Magic shot from her fingers as she tried to get me off her, but it was no use. The binding magic wouldn't let her kill me. Plus, I was too close and I had too strong of a grip.

Her eyes grew to large, round circles and her face turned red, but all I saw was a woman that needed to die a long time ago. When she kicked and scratched me, I squeezed even tighter. I squeezed until her hands got weak and all the strength had left her. Her body fell limp in my arms and finally I released her, lowering her to the couch where she could take her final rest.

After I'd learned she'd murdered Lily, she'd become the worst kind of monster in my mind. Somehow, her lifeless body didn't seem so monstrous now. For the briefest moment, I wondered if I should have forgiven her. I'd known her for centuries and I hadn't always hated her. Her love for me turned into a twisted kind of obsession, driving her to kill those I loved, and for what? Because she thought I would love her when they were out of the picture? I couldn't wrap my head around that way of thinking.

Maybe now that she was gone, some part of me could forgive the monster that she was. But I could never forgive what she'd done.

I opened the door and found Guido leaning against the far wall and staring at his phone. His eyebrows rose when he saw me; he scanned behind me, looking for Ixia.

"She's dead, buddy," I said.

He caught a glimpse of her lying on the couch and turned to me as if to attack. I flung him back with a sweep of my hand, plastering him against the wall. I strolled past him and released my hold as soon as I opened the door. I could hear his body thump on the ground as I left.

I picked up my pace as I navigated the maze out of the villa. When I finally got out of there, I ran toward the garden where I could teleport without being seen. Suddenly, I heard someone call my name in the distance. I turned, ready to stop whoever was there with my magic, and froze in my tracks when I saw who it was. "Vera?"

She was hiding behind a large redwood tree, Jayce, the accountant rebel whom we'd met at Jultin's recording studio crouched beside her.

"Come quick," she called.

As I approached her, I could tell something was wrong. "Your leg."

She had a bloody, makeshift bandage around her thigh, and I imagined there was a huge slash beneath the fabric.

"Jayce and his small rebel army helped me get to my sister and her family. They were being held nearby. I was able to set them free and get them to the safe house, but I got in a fight with one of Balastar's Zolless on the way there. He managed to get in a small cut on my leg. When we got to the safe house, Jayce was there waiting for me. He suspected you were here and told me we should come get you out. But the cut got infected, fast. It was a small cut just a little while ago, but now I can't move."

I lifted her with my arm and supported returned to the accountant who no longer looked like an accountant. He had traded his suit for camouflage gear and was strapped with a gun on his belt. "Thank you for coming," I said.

"The stars write the path," he said, and gave Vera a look of concern. "I'm going to leave her with you now. I've got to get back to my people. They're fighting on the front line."

"Jayce," I called after him. "In the safe of Jultin's apartment there is a poison that neutralizes Fae magic. There's more in Ixia's laboratory. Take what you need then destroy that place so her potions don't get in the wrong hands." I handed him the key to Jultin's safe. He took it and gave me a slight nod, then he ran off.

"We're getting you out of here," I told Vera. I teleported us to the back of the Aquarius Zol Sen monastery where the zodiac wheel was kept.

"Damian! Vera!" I heard Sasha call when we arrived. I smiled as I saw Lex, Jenna and Eliana there with Sasha. Bloodied Zol Council soldiers' bodies littered the floor.

Sasha rushed forward. "Balastar told me what was happening and I came as soon as I heard. We had to clear the guards that were protecting the zodiac wheel so you could transit to Aries."

I simply nodded. "Thanks. We need to get her to a healer, fast. She's lost a lot of blood." Vera's head slumped on my shoulder and her body felt weak.

"Wait for my sister," Vera said, her eyes fixed on me.

"Where is she?" I asked.

"I can feel her. She's close. I told her to come to the zodiac wheel and meet me." She craned her head to look out the windows.

I went to work on Vera's leg. I wasn't a healer, but I knew some spells that could stop the infection from spreading. "It looks like we can save the leg. This will help until we can get you to a healer."

Lex was on watch at the windows for the arrival of Vera's family. Finally, after the sun began to set, an elven woman approached the building with her two young children.

"Hey, Vera. Take a look. Is that her?" he asked.

Vera lifted her gaze hopefully. "Yes!"

As Lex escorted them into the room, the woman cried, "Vera!" She went to her sister and held her hands. Vera gave her a comforting smile in return and reached for her niece and nephew. They hugged her lightly, as though in a shocked kind of sadness.

"We came where you told us," the elf said. "It took us a while; we had a few soldiers trailing us that we had to lose in the forest." She looked just as tough as Vera, and so did her two children.

"You did well. Where's Glendal?" Vega asked.

The elven woman shook her head sadly.

"It's time to go," Sasha said.

Vera's sister held her tight as the nagual led us through safe passage back to Aries.

CHAPTER 30

SIX MONTHS LATER

"Jayce Arion," I heard the news reporter say at campaign headquarters. I started jumping up and down with excitement. I high-fived all the people around me and raced over to Jayce to give him a hug. "Congratulations!"

He returned my hug. "Thank you, my queen. For believing in me and helping me get here. I wouldn't have done it without you and the nagual forces."

I didn't know what a queen would say in this situation, but I gave it my best shot. "You honor me." I placed my hand on my chest and beamed at him. "A crowd is forming and I'm sure the others will want to congratulate you, too."

He nodded and I quickly moved out of the way as the rest of his campaign team went to him. When the commotion settled down, we joined him on the stadium stage where his supporters filled every seat.

I shot a glance at Balastar, who gave me a supportive nod, and approached the microphone. There I stood before the thousands of people in attendance. "Tonight, I bring you the first ever elected officer of Zol Stria. He won in a landslide victory and his opponents have told me they wouldn't have wanted to lose to anyone else." The cheers and laughs reverberated throughout the stadium. His opponents were all there, watching from the stage with us. I gestured to the eleven of them.

"Balastar and I will be working closely with Jayce to establish the new ruling structure for the twelve Houses, and elections will follow for each territory. I have a strong feeling we'll be seeing more of these guys very soon." I turned to face the other candidates and clapped. The crowd clapped for them, too. "Now, I give you Jayce Arion, Prime Minister of Zol Stria."

Jayce approached the microphone. His suit was crisp, his haircut trim, and his face groomed perfectly for this very moment. "First of all, this celebration is for our queen, Sasha Moreno. She sacrificed everything and led us to freedom. We are fortunate to have her as a leader and I hope to count on many years of your involvement in our restructuring and revival."

As the crowd erupted with cheers and excitement, I felt whole. So often in my life I had wondered what my purpose was and why the stars had led me down the paths I had been on. But every single step had led me in this direction. I was exactly where I needed to be, and I was completely fulfilled.

"I would also like to thank everyone who voted for me in this historical election," Jayce continued. "For the first time in our thousands of years of history, all Fae will be seen, heard and represented by our laws. There will no longer be the marginalization of our people. No more slavery. No more taking of firstborns or lack of regard for the life of any Fae."

The crowd cheered and kept cheering and celebrating long into the night.

One moon after Damian had returned to us, the war had turned in our favor. The remaining seven Houses had sent word that they would be willing to negotiate. Yet the rulers decided not to show up at the day and time we had agreed upon so we set another date. They refused to show up to that date, too, instead launching a surprise attack on our stronghold in Libra. So when the moon was high in the sky, I visited the home of the Queen of House Capricorn.

She was swimming in her palace pool, and as I approached, I was met with a dark shadow that attempted to slice a knife through my battle gear and straight into my heart. I shifted into my jaguar form, ripping my battle gear off me, my fangs thirsty for the blood of this queen.

I dodged the blow just in time, for Balastar had warned me he would be there. This was one of the very few nagual loyalists who had remained with the Council.

Behind me, heat flooded off Balastar. Startled, I turned around and watched him shift into another form with such grace I had never seen. Bright, fiery wings exploded from his back. He grew to twice his normal height, his form shifting as he glowed in awesome beauty. I took several steps back. There had never before been a phoenix shifter. They were supposed to be a myth.

He was crimson and gold and inexplicably beautiful. His gift of sight allowed him to see the shadows, and he took my nagual attacker by surprise when he gripped his shadow form with his huge red talons. A tortured scream escaped the dark mist and filled the air. Balastar squeezed until the nagual returned to his Zol skin, then squeezed some more until

I heard bones snap and his screams cease. It was strange to watch one of our own kind on the other side of our fight, even stranger to watch them die.

As I saw the nagual's blood spill into the pool.

"And from the ashes, the phoenix will rise."

I'd read this quote in a book several times. There was a famous phoenix statue in Capricorn Gate and a prophecy that a phoenix would come to this world in the sign of Capricorn. Balastar had returned from the Void as a Capricorn. The phoenix suited him. He had risen from the Void, after all, the darkest of ashes.

"Ahhhhh," the queen in the water screamed as the nagual's blood dripped into the pool.

I dove into the water and she barely put up a fight. Her thin arms had never had to protect her before and she had no tangible self-defense training. It was almost too simple to form a knife from my shadows and slit her throat, turning the water bright red in the process.

Once word got out of the queen's death, the Zol Council agreed to meet with us the very next day with all the remaining rulers present. The six living kings and queens, along with those recently promoted to second-in-line, were able to formalize an agreement with us to dismember the Zol Council and form a new structure with equal numbers of elected members from the Dark Fae.

This was a huge step forward and the rulers wanted to make us agree not to kill any more of them if we didn't agree with something they did. We were happy to do so, so long as the rulers who had committed murder, had taken Fae into slavery and had abused the lower Fae would be tried before a court of their peers.

They weren't happy about that at all, but they came to realize that at this point they didn't have a choice. We would keep coming for them until they were all dead if we had to.

That night as we were celebrating the momentous election, I found Damian and Vera sitting closely on a couch in the lounge where we were all enjoying the festivities. He was staring lovingly in her eyes, and my heart filled with joy as I realized how happy he truly was.

Damian had finally found love again and with someone who loved him in return. He was free to enjoy his time with her without the psycho-ex-girlfriend drama that had plagued him for so long. I had his commitment, and that of my entire nagual family, that we would all stay here in Aries for the next forty years to establish the new order of Zol

Stria and plan the introduction of zodiac magic slowly into the mortal world. It would be a long process, but it was the natural order of things. It had to happen to restore balance in both of our worlds. I was just glad I was going to be able to do it all with the people I loved.

As the night came to a close, I returned to Balastar who was quietly sitting on the balcony that overlooked Lake Aries. The moon's reflection was bright on the lake and I couldn't take my eyes off it.

"I'm so glad Jayce won," I told him.

"Was there any doubt?" Balastar chuckled.

"No, I guess not. He's got a big job restructuring Zol Stria now that the Council has been dissolved. I'm confident he can handle it, especially with all of us to support him."

"The stars write the path," Balastar said and reached for my hand. Although Balastar was the clear ruler of the Dark Fae, Jayce represented both sides of Zol Stria. There were still many loyalists of the Zol Council who were very skeptical of the UnZol King's interest in the welfare of all people. Jayce was a more neutral leader who had the ability to unite people from both sides under his leadership. Balastar and I agreed it was best if he was the face of all Zol Stria.

My expression turned serious. "The first order of business is to get the Zolless under control. We need to do it now, before they cause any more harm."

"I've already done it, mi amor," he said. I locked eyes with him, expecting him to say more. "I've been hunting them almost every night. As a phoenix, my eyesight is incredible. I've plucked them one by one from this world. There are no more Zolless to worry about."

"So that's where you've been going! I was wondering why I wouldn't see you for hours. I thought you were meeting with the war generals in the different territories."

"I did meet with them. But when I was done, I would scour the land."

My expression softened and I gave him smile. He pulled me toward him and I sat on his lap. "So that's why there aren't any reports of their attacks. But why didn't you tell me? I would have been glad to know this."

"I wanted to tell you when it was done so it would be a surprise. I know how you love surprises." He chuckled.

"I do love surprises, but next time, tell me. If anything would have happened to you..."

The side of his mouth twisted up into a half-smile. "Really? Something happen to me?"

"You never know!" I gave him a light shove before tracing my fingers along the full hairs of his beard. I felt my body grow warm just touching him.

"I guess being a phoenix makes you sort of invincible," I said out loud as I stared at him in wonder. I mean at least I hoped it did. I never wanted to be separated from him again. He was my Zol Mate and we needed to spend an eternity together.

"Well, I guess you could say that." His gaze was focused on me and all I wanted to do was get lost in those eyes. "I asked the Master Zol Sen about this new form. I wanted to know why I lost my dragon and what they knew about the Phoenix. There's never been a Pheonix, so they didn't have much information on the form. But no one has ever returned from the Void before, either. But the theory is that if I should be killed, I will rise again." I started laughing. "Let's not try and find out, ok?"

He laughed with me and said, "I'll try."

"When you came from the Void, you had no beard, but you also had no way to shave if you did grow one. Now it's grown in all the way. Why is that?" I asked.

"Ah, the important questions in life, like how does one grow a beard in the Void." He chuckled, and I giggled. "I guess I stayed exactly the way I went in, and back then I didn't have a beard."

"Makes sense. I'm glad you grew it in. I like it."

It was strange being with him without the stress of our world's worries on our shoulders. Strange, but in a good way.

"Now that I think about it, there is one agreement that we made to Vera that we haven't fulfilled," he said.

"What?"

"The making of an heir."

I threw my head back and laughed. "Then we better get to work."

CHAPTER 31

DIMITRI, DEMON WAITER OF THE UNDERWORLD PALACE

When the rulers of the Great Houses of Zol Stria fell, the death god Vucub-Cane invited his brother Hun-Cane for dinner. His brother arrived at the death god's Underworld palace in a fitted black suit with a subtle sheen that could only be seen when the light hit it.

He entered the palace and was welcomed by Vucub-Cane himself, who approached him with a sly grin on his face. His suit was also perfectly fitted and as white as his hair.

"You certainly out did yourself this time, brother," Hun-Cane said.

Vucub-Cane couldn't help but gloat. "This one was at least two thousand years in the making. I have to admit, it was genius. And now you've got to pay up."

"Fine. For the next thousand years, the souls of all the dead are yours," Hun-Cane conceded begrudgingly. "But you've got to give me a chance to earn them back."

"Let's discuss it over dinner," Vucub-Cane said. He placed his hand lightly on his brother's shoulder as they strolled casually to their dining table. As gods they had no need of food, but they enjoyed the taste of Chef Amari's cooking so much that they dined anyway.

ACKNOWLEDGEMENTS

As you read the pages of the Warrior Shifter series, you were experiencing the manifestation of one of my biggest dreams. The idea of that, still gives me goosebumps. There have been many highs and lows throughout the process, and I am just as grateful for the lows as I am the highs. And sometimes the lows Sasha experienced, ran parallel to my own. And sometimes I used her lows as an outlet and release for much of the emotional mess I was in. No matter how low I may have ever felt while writing the hard parts that Sasha had to overcome, there were those people that kept lifting me up. Especially you, the readers. Your downloads, reviews and shares of these books have kept me motivated and inspired the whole way through.

I have to thank my amazing husband who never let me doubt myself, not even for one second. My three wonderful daughters, who each believed in my writing and wanted me to see this project all the way through. And there were my dear friends, that supported me through the whole entire process. I am so incredibly grateful to have had the opportunity to work on this series. My life is richer because I got to experience the roller coaster ride that has been writing and publishing these books.

Thanks to my amazing editor, Shavonne Clark, this entire series reached an even higher level of storytelling. Her creative ideas, clarifying questions and masterful wordsmithing made all the difference. I'm so grateful for my beta readers, Jessica Fraser and Nola Barr, who delivered exceptional insight right when I needed it. And to my amazing cover designers at Miblart, for their beautiful creative designs. A very special thank you to Kristen Raspberry, who has been such a great supporter of my books and an amazing cheerleader that I now consider a friend.

I am so grateful to have been able to get to know so many amazing people in the process of creating these books, while expanding my mind and creativity in ways I never even imagined. My heart is full.

THE WARRIOR SHIFTER SERIES

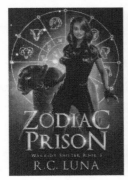

ABOUT THE AUTHOR

R.C. Luna is a moon child who believes we are all made of stardust.

Her passion for books, magic, witchcraft and mystery comes alive with the sexy, paranormal monsters that line the pages of her books. Her characters are driven by the phases of the moon and the alignment of the stars.

Luna's experience as a Puerto Rican growing up in South Florida influences her writing of multicultural storylines, as does her time spent in the U.S. Air Force and living in several different Latin American countries.

Darkness is her playground, and you'll find her up well into the night reading fantasy romance novels.

Sign up for her newsletter and receive the FREE prequel – Zodiac Shadows, along with updates on the latest releases in her series, *Warrior Shifter* and free fantasy books from great authors on the regular.

www.rcluna.com

KEEP IN TOUCH

www.rcluna.com

Facebook @authorrcluna
Instagram @author_rcluna
Join my Facebook Group

Made in the USA
Coppell, TX
04 February 2025

45432110R00088